Dear Reader,

I don't necessarily believe in paranormal signs, but sometimes it's hard to ignore them. When starting this book, I fretted about the challenge of writing about twins and took a break for—what else—shopping. At the mall, a woman passed by with adorable twin girls about four years old, sitting side by side in a stroller. They were dressed in identical pink jumpers with their blond curls in matching hairstyles. As a writer, it was a profound moment for me because I hadn't thought about my characters as children, but I started to. It was a sign.

Not long after, I visited a friend who also had twin girls. I asked one of them (Kim? Kelly?) whether or not they ever switched places to fool teachers or friends. The answer was no, because they were too shy. This also gave me an insight into the type of personality that would take on the challenge of pretending to be someone else. The final piece of Beth's character fell into place with something their mother told me. Only to protect her sister would either of her twins do something as drastic as changing identities. It was a sign.

It does make me wonder about fate and why certain people cross our path at just the right time. In *The Sheikh's Contract Bride* a betrothal is what sets romance in motion, but the woman who becomes the sheikh's bride is all about destiny. I hope you enjoy reading Malik and Beth's story as much as I enjoyed writing it.

Teresa Southwick

"I will kiss you. And soon."

"Oh?" The single syllable was almost a squeak.

"When it happens, I wish it to mean something."

It would mean that she was going straight to hell. Do not pass go. Do not collect her wings and halo. She was going to lose her soul.

"When it happens," he continued, "it will be because you cannot get me out of your mind. When our lips finally touch, you will feel it everywhere. The meeting of our mouths will be so sweet and deep and passionate that you will never want it to end."

TERESA SOUTHWICK

The Sheikh's Contract Bride

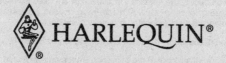

TORONTO • NEW YORK • LONDON
AMSTERDAM • PARIS • SYDNEY • HAMBURG
STOCKHOLM • ATHENS • TOKYO • MILAN • MADRID
PRAGUE • WARSAW • BUDAPEST • AUCKLAND

ISBN-13: 978-0-373-03957-9
ISBN-10:   0-373-03957-3

THE SHEIKH'S CONTRACT BRIDE

First North American Publication 2007.

Copyright © 2007 by Teresa Ann Southwick.

This edition published by arrangement with Harlequin Books S.A.

® and TM are trademarks of the publisher. Trademarks indicated with
® are registered in the United States Patent and Trademark Office, the
Canadian Trade Marks Office and in other countries.

www.eHarlequin.com

Printed in U.S.A.

Teresa Southwick has written over twenty-five books, and calls writing the best job in the world. She lives in Las Vegas, where she's hard at work on her next romance novel.

Teresa Southwick on *The Sheikh's Contract Bride*

"I love books about arranged marriages. As a writer, I had a very wonderful time with poor Malik. He is only too willing to do the right thing and marry the woman chosen by his father, but the fun comes when not only does he fall hard, but also the woman he's in love with turns out to be his betrothed's identical twin. What's a sheikh to do?"

Brothers of Bha'Khar

In April you met younger brother Kardahl in

The Sheikh's Reluctant Bride

This month it's the turn of Malik, the heir of Bha'Khar, to find his rightful bride!

To Judi McCoy for always being there.
And Sandra Ferguson for the same reason.

CHAPTER ONE

SINCE she was headed for the seventh level of hell, now would be a good time to sunscreen her soul.

Alina Bethia Farrah knew truth was the best way to avoid the burning issues of the afterlife. And she'd admit to not always valuing honesty as much as she should have. But, as much as she hated pretending, she'd made a promise to switch places with her identical twin and stand up to the man her sister couldn't—His Royal Highness, Malik Hourani, the Crown Prince of Bha'Khar.

Beth had only ever had her sister to count on, and Adina was the only person who had ever loved her. Her request was the emotional equivalent of bleeding or being on fire. Saying no wasn't an option.

But now that Beth was here in the palace, waiting to meet the Prince, the reckless spirit that had convinced her she could pull this off completely wimped out. As she stared at her suitcases lined up on the exquisite marble floor of the entryway, the deception that in her L.A. apartment had felt noble—wrong thing, right reason—now just seemed wrong.

She was pretending to be the woman who was going to marry the sheikh because her sister wanted out of the marriage agreement.

As the firstborn by two minutes, Addie had been betrothed by their father, the Bha'Kharian ambassador to the United States, to the royal heir. Now, Addie was torn between being disowned by the father she adored or marrying a man she'd never met. Neither alternative was appealing, especially after she'd begun dating a man—possibly *the* man.

It had been several years since she'd come of age, and she'd begun to hope the sheikh had forgotten their arrangement. But only a few weeks ago he'd begun the process of finalizing their betrothal with wedding vows—and he wanted to do it sooner rather than later. That was when Addie had come up with the idea of switching places.

Outspoken Beth had often run interference for introspective Addie when they were children, and had assumed her identity. But this wasn't about which twin had broken the lamp or hadn't eaten her brussels sprouts. This secret could have international repercussions.

Beth didn't like secrets. But she liked her sister's situation even less. Beth had once fallen for a guy like the sheikh, a man from a politically connected family who believed it was perfectly all right to be married and have a mistress. He felt entitled to play by different rules because he was a powerful man. Now her sister was engaged to one of the world's most powerful men, and Beth could only imagine what rules *he* lived by. This arranged marriage was just wrong, and somehow Beth would get Addie out of it.

Now she waited for the Crown Prince in the apartment where the royal intended, or in this case her facsimile, would stay until the wedding. Nervous, Beth paced and checked out the place. The living room was spacious and bright, and filled with expensive art—paintings, blown glass, and figurines. French doors opened onto a balcony overlooking the Arabian Sea, and when she pulled the doors wide the breeze blowing off the ocean cooled her hot cheeks.

She could do this. She and her twin were interchangeable; no one could tell them apart, not even their father. This should be as easy as falling off a log, especially with a guy who'd never met either of them.

The knock on the apartment door startled her, even though she'd been expecting it—maybe *because* she'd been expecting it.

Letting out a long breath, she walked through the apartment, then opened the door—and stared like a fool. The man standing there was tall and dark and—Wow. Handsome was an understatement.

Pulling herself together, she said, "Hi."

"I am Malik Hourani." With the barest movement of his shoulders and head, he executed a respectful bow.

"The Prince?"

"Indeed," he said.

"How do you do?"

"I do very well." His dark eyes glowed with male approval. "Although I regret that I was not there when your plane arrived."

"Technically, it's your plane."

"That is true," he said seriously. "But I did want to greet you and was unable to do so."

"That's all right." She'd been relieved. "I was told that you'd be tied up with business until this evening."

"Things went better than I had expected and I am grateful as I was eager to meet you. Welcome to Bha'Khar, Adina Farrah."

First hurdle crossed. At first sight he believed she was Addie. Her heart started thumping really hard. She had no more time to prepare herself. Here he was in the flesh. And very nice flesh it was—what she could see of it. The expensive black suit hid a lot, although it fit his tall, muscular body perfectly. His lean cheeks and straight nose were exceptionally attractive. But it was his mouth that mesmerized her and, she suspected, commanded the attention of any female who was still breathing. There was an innate sensuality to his lips, a defined curve as if carved from stone, yet they were soft with the promise of passion.

Beth had never met a man who instantly made her want to know what his mouth would feel like against her own. Not until now. That was definitely a distraction, and she so didn't need it. She needed to keep her wits sharp and come up with a plausible reason for him to call her by a name she would actually answer to.

"Hardly anyone calls me Adina," she said.

"Why?"

Good question. And this was where the truth worked.

"Everyone calls me Beth, for Bethia."

"Oh?"

She nodded. "It's my middle name. Our parents didn't think it through when my sister and I were named. Adina. Alina." She shrugged.

"You are twins."

"We are." Her heart pounded as she waited for him to recognize her deception, even though there was no reason for him to suspect anything. When he waited patiently, she said, "You can imagine the confusion when our names sound so much alike. So I became Beth." Always best to go with as much of the truth as possible.

"Is that how you would prefer to be addressed?"

"Yes."

He nodded. "Then Beth is what I shall call you."

"Thank you, Your Highness."

"Please call me Malik. I wish to put you at ease."

So he *had* noticed her nerves. Hopefully he'd chalk it up to the circumstances. "Being an ambassador's daughter, I learned the proper form of address for distinguished persons at an early age. It's difficult for me to relax old habits and training."

"That is understandable. Think of it this way.

Sometimes I am called His Royal Highness. Sometimes Sir. Occasionally I am called things not fit to repeat in front of a lady." He grinned suddenly, showing very white teeth against his tanned skin. "However, in private, as we are now, my given name is preferable."

Was it her imagination or had his voice dropped and become sexier on the word private? Was it also her imagination that the oxygen in this room had suddenly thinned, making her want to take long, deep breaths?

"Malik it is, then," she said, trying to relax. "It's a pleasure to finally meet you."

"The pleasure is mine, Beth." He held out his hand.

She put hers into his palm and felt the warmth and strength of his long fingers. Then the tingles started. They danced up her arm and settled in her breasts, as if he were touching her there. His dark eyes turned smoky and intense, as if he felt the same flash of heat.

"Yes. Okay. Introductions accomplished," she said, pulling her hand from his. Again she couldn't think straight. It was as if touching him short-circuited her brain functions.

"Indeed." He nodded toward the other room. "Let us sit and relax, get to know one another."

"All right."

She backed away from him, then turned and went into the living room, grateful that she made it all the way to the sofa without her legs giving out. Relaxing wasn't going to happen. She had a feeling that even if she wasn't pretending to be her sister she'd be a fool to let down her guard around this man. The aura of confidence and power surrounding him—the very qualities that had landed her in trouble before—were compelling and exciting.

"I wish you to tell me everything about yourself," he said.

Was that an order? The imperious tone touched a nerve before the words sank in. "But we're betrothed. Don't you already know everything?"

He unbuttoned his suit coat, revealing a snow-white shirt and flat abdomen. Then he sat a foot away and met her gaze. "It is impossible to know everything. I know you were raised in the United States until attending boarding school in Switzerland and college in France, where you received a degree in Art History. I know we are betrothed because your father is my father's trusted ambassador and friend. May I ask how he is?"

"Fine." The last time she'd seen him, and she couldn't remember when that was.

"I am pleased that he is well. He has assured me of your impeccable background and speaks very highly of you. But I have been supplied only with details."

The devil was in the details. She hated this, and it was on the tip of her tongue to tell him what was going on, but she decided to wait. "Well, I don't know what to say." And that was definitely the truth.

He met her gaze and his own darkened. "I prefer to act as if we had met by chance. I wish the facets of your individuality to be revealed as we indulge in the dance of learning about each other. I like surprises."

That was good. If he ever found out she wasn't who he thought, he was in for a big surprise. The thing was, when she and Addie were kids, who dressed alike and wore their hair in identical styles, it had been far easier to fool everyone. They'd both gone to finishing school, but Beth had become a teacher and Addie could throw a formal dinner party for the population of a small country.

"Prepare to be surprised," she said. If her cover was blown and the pretense stopped here, Addie would pay a high price. The best plan was to tell the truth when at all possible. "I'm a teacher—high school English." And this ruse was how she was spending her summer vacation.

"That is a detail I did not know. So you have a career?"

"Yes."

"Do you like teaching?" His expression appeared to be one of genuine interest, not an aha-you're-lying-and-now-you're-busted look.

"Yes."

"And children?"

"I like them very much. Why do you ask?"

"Because I am expected to produce an heir to the throne."

"Then *you* be pregnant and go through child-birth." The words popped out of her mouth before she could stop them. Her sister wouldn't have slipped up like that.

He frowned. "You do not want children?"

"Someday I'd like to be a mother." But she didn't expect it to happen. Not without love. And she really didn't expect that.

"Will you miss it when we are married?"

"What?"

"Teaching. Your career."

So it was expected that being his bride would be a full-time job, one for which her sister had been exquisitely trained. But he'd asked *her*, Beth, and she'd worked hard. She loved her job and felt she really connected with the teenagers she taught. "I have to be honest."

"I expect nothing less."

"I would miss it very much. Is that a problem?"

He sat back as he thought. "It is a bridge we will cross when the time comes."

Spoken like a powerful politician, she thought. Translation: we'll do it my way, and it doesn't matter if your heart gets broken. The woman he married would be subject to this attitude. But Beth wasn't the woman he was supposed to marry, thank goodness.

"Later works for me," she said.

"What do you think of Bha'Khar?"

"I haven't seen much yet," she admitted. "But I remember going to the open-air market when I was a child. My mother used to—"

She had a sudden, vivid vision of smells and sights and sounds, and the safe, secure feeling of her hand in her mother's. The emptiness inside her was like a black hole that swallowed up all the light. A part of her had stayed empty ever since her mother had abandoned her and Addie to be raised by a stern, autocratic father. The scandal and abandonment had devastated Beth, but her twin had taken it even harder.

"What is it?" he asked.

"Nothing." The knot in her stomach said different, but this wasn't the right time to discuss it. While she was in the country she planned to see her mother and tell her to her face exactly what she thought about someone who would abandon her children. And, more than that, Beth wanted to know why she'd done it.

Speaking of interrogations, Malik was asking most of the questions. It was time to take the heat off herself and learn about him. For Addie's agenda to extricate herself from this contract, she told herself, not her own reluctant curiosity about a man who had shown a romantic streak in that "dance of learning about each other" remark.

"Tell me about you," she said.

He thought for a moment. "I will soon be the King. From birth, I have been in training to assume the throne and lead my country and my people into more prosperity than we currently enjoy. My father has been a great example and has challenged me continuously to surpass him."

"Where did you go to college?"

The question slipped out before she could stop it. That information was readily available if she had cared to look. She hoped he was not offended that she hadn't bothered to find out.

"I was educated at the Wharton School, one of the most prestigious business colleges in the eastern United States. I have a Master's Degree in Economics."

Very impressive, she thought. So he was smart. That would help in running the country. It wouldn't help on the attraction front. A smart, good-looking man with a sense of humor was too easy to like.

"What are your intentions toward my—" She stopped and cleared her throat. "Toward me. I mean, what do you expect of a wife?"

"This is beginning to sound like a job interview," he said.

"Really? Have you ever had a job interview?"

"Why do you ask?"

She shrugged. "Since you're first in the line of succession, you have the position in the bag, so to speak. How would you know what it feels like to be interrogated about your ability—or lack thereof—to do a job?"

"You are correct. There is no interview. Which is why the successor to the King is held to a higher standard. More is expected."

"Is the same expected of a husband? And what about the woman you marry? Since she—I—was born into it, does that mean she—I—have to work harder at being a wife?"

He frowned. "I had not thought about it."

"Newsflash, Your Highness, the clock is ticking. It's time to think about it."

Malik detected an edge in her voice. Not only

that, he had noticed immediately that she was nervous. It was evident in the tightness of her mouth, the hooded expression in her light brown eyes and the swiftness with which she had removed her hand from his when he'd introduced himself.

In another woman he would have taken it as proof of a hidden agenda. After being played for a fool and betrayed by such a woman, he was wary of pretenders. But Beth had reason for this show of anxiety. Meeting her betrothed for the first time was worthy of an acute case of nerves.

He had to admit to some nervousness himself. He had only seen her in photographs. Beauty was not a requirement for his bride; truthfulness and integrity were of more importance. However, he had been exceedingly pleased by her features.

He liked the shiny dark hair that framed her oval face and fell to her slender shoulders. The silk blouse tucked into the small waist of her suit pants clung to her breasts and highlighted her pleasing curves. But that was not all that had surprised him. There was a strength about her that had not been apparent in the pictures passed on to him by her father.

The eight-by-ten photographs did not capture the three-dimensional woman. The warmth. Vibrancy. The spirit that had flashed in her eyes when she'd said the clock was ticking on their betrothal.

"Do you feel too hurried in the business of this marriage?" he asked. "I do not wish to create excessive pressure."

"I've always known about it," she said, speaking

slowly and apparently choosing her words with care. "But there was no firm date."

By his own choice. He had lost his heart to a woman who had pretended to be something she was not. His error in judgment had nearly been made public and it had been necessary to inform the King. The incident had embarrassed him personally and professionally, and, worse, had deeply disappointed his father. The poor judgment he had exhibited had cast doubt on his ability to be an effective leader. Afterwards, Malik had not wanted an emotional commitment of any kind. He would have put off taking vows indefinitely, except that it was a way to prove he would commit everything to his duty. Unlike women, duty was constant and without pretense.

"My father has expressed his wish to retire. He wants me to assume leadership responsibilities as soon as possible."

"I see." Sitting on the edge of the sofa, she folded her hands in her lap. "But you could be King and take over the government without getting married? Right?"

"You are correct. But, as I said before, it is my duty to produce an heir to the throne and the child must be legitimate. That requires marriage."

A fact the King had pointed out when Malik had attempted to delay the inevitable. His father had also firmly stated that marriage gave a man stability and dignity, both of which were desirable qualities in an effective ruler. Because his bride had been selected based on impeccable lineage, and raised to be obedient, to put her patriotic duty before personal pursuits, there would be no chance of another embarrassing incident.

However, Beth was a teacher, and that detail had not come to his attention. Her father had no doubt felt it unimportant, but Malik disagreed. It boded well for her maternal skills—a desirable trait in the woman who would bear his children.

"Still, what's the rush?" she asked.

"Besides the King's retirement? It is simply time to fulfill our destiny, and yours is to be the Queen of Bha'Khar. To take your place by my side in the service of our people."

Her big eyes grew bigger. "Oh, wow—"

"Something troubles you?"

"Yeah. Queen of Bha'Khar? That's a pretty overwhelming thought." Something akin to panic stirred in her gaze.

"I do not understand. As you said, you've always known what was in your future."

"Yes." She stood. "But knowing and doing are two different things. Kind of like being exposed to the flu, then losing your lunch."

He stood and looked down at her. "I understand that a good deal of your experience and upbringing happened in the United States, and Americans are more casual. It is one of their most unique and charming qualities. But I wish to make certain I understand what you are saying."

"I'm sorry." She sighed. "That came out a bit

harsher than I intended. I simply meant that it's one thing to know what's going to happen and quite another to actually go through the steps. Like being condemned—"

He held up his hand. "You are not making it better."

"Sorry."

"May I ask you a question?"

"Do you have to?"

He refused to be distracted by her teasing or her beauty. "In all of your instruction on protocol, diplomacy, and etiquette, were you ever once told that it was politically incorrect to compare royal life to the flu or a death sentence?"

Her chin lifted slightly as she said, "I'd like to be clear on something as well."

"I am happy to discuss anything with you." He noticed that she had not answered his question. "What is it you wish to know?"

"Are you really all right with having your bride picked out for you? Like a tie? Or a pair of shoes?"

"You are hardly a tie."

She started pacing. "But you know what I mean. What if we don't get along? What if I snore? What if we don't get each other's sense of humor? What if you don't have one? What if—"

He held up a hand. "Clearly you have reservations about the betrothal."

"Yes," she said with great feeling. "Don't you?"

"No."

She had been chosen and educated in the proper behavior of the wife of the King. Together they would guide this country into a powerful position in the global community. That was all he needed to know. And she had not once mentioned the matter that he would have expected a woman with doubts to bring up.

"Are you not concerned about love?" he asked.

"No." Her tone was rife with unexpected passion.

"You do not wish to be in love?"

"Not even for money," she confirmed. But her gaze lowered just before she turned away and started pacing again. "Love is not all it's cracked up to be."

"I agree." He knew why *he* did not wish to experience the emotion again, but he was most curious to know what had poisoned her against it.

"That's good."

"Yes. Accord is something to be treasured between a man and his wife. That bodes well for—"

"Wait."

"What?" he asked.

"Just because neither of us wants to be in love it doesn't get us on the same planet with accord. Love is simply one issue. There are billions of things to think about."

"Again, I agree. After we are married we will have the rest of our lives to work out these things."

She stopped in front of him. "And there's my point. A man and woman contemplating spending the rest of their lives together usually work the big stuff out before they get engaged."

"Royalty is different."

Her look was wry. "No kidding."

"Is your father aware of your misgivings? Have you discussed this with him?"

Her gaze skittered away. "He's more into issuing proclamations and orders than in having actual discussions," she answered, which was not an answer at all.

"If you do not accept the time-honored tradition of this betrothal, then why did you come all this way to marry me?"

"That's the thing," she said. Her gaze was direct when she met his. "I came all this way to talk you out of it."

CHAPTER TWO

"YOU came halfway around the world to change my mind about an honored Bha'Kharian tradition?"

Beth winced when he put it like that. She'd come because her sister had begged her. Addie needed time to figure out how to break off the engagement without alienating their father. Anything less than blind obedience would result in being cut out of his life as if she'd never existed. Addie was terrified to take that step and close the door on her relationship with the only parent she had.

Beth wasn't as docile as her sister and said what was on her mind—a flaw that had already damaged her relationship with her father. Raised without a mother, she understood why Addie was desperate to preserve her remaining family connections. If not for her sister, Beth would have grown up in an emotional vacuum. She'd have no blueprint for love. Granted, she'd been burned by the emotion, but better to have loved and lost, as the saying went. She couldn't stand by and do nothing when the sister who'd taught her to love might be cut off from it.

Talking Malik out of this tradition made perfect sense for everyone. Putting herself in his shoes— knowing that his bride had been chosen and he'd had no say in the matter—maybe she had a better than even chance of making him see reason. For God's sake, he was going to be King. Shouldn't he have a choice about the woman who would help him shoulder that responsibility?

She looked up at him. "Sometimes change is good. Shake things up."

"Sometimes the old ways are better."

"All right," she said, tapping her lip. "But you never answered my question about whether or not you're okay with not choosing your own bride."

"There are advantages to letting others with nothing clouding their objectivity do the picking."

"Picking?" She put her hands on her hips as she met his gaze. "You make me sound like a ripe plum."

"On the contrary, plums are sweeter and more docile. Aside from those two things—" he shrugged "—I am well pleased with the selection my father made."

Beth didn't know if she'd just been complimented or insulted. Or both.

"Well, of course you're pleased. What's not to like?"

"Please explain." He folded his arms over his chest and gave her his full attention.

"An arranged marriage works in your favor because you're a powerful man."

He shook his head. "I do not understand what that has to do with anything."

Was he deliberately being obtuse? "Being in a position of power means you get to control everything. You can set the rules. Nothing about this situation works in *my* favor."

"Nothing?" He frowned. "Do you find me unattractive?"

"No." What she wanted to say was *Good God, no.* "You're very handsome."

One corner of his mouth lifted. "Does my personality displease you?"

"Since we just met, it's too soon to tell. So far you seem okay."

He nodded. "Is the palace not to your liking? You object to living here?"

"Oh, please. What I've seen of it is gorgeous, and you know it."

"Then I am at a loss to understand your objections."

"My objections have to do with the fact that there's more to marriage than pleasing looks, personality and a palace." When put like that, it occurred to her that perhaps her standards were a tad high. "There's something to be said for a normal courtship."

"Define this for me."

The fact that he needed a definition for normal should have been a big clue. But she was supposed to be impersonating her sister, and Adina was nothing if not cooperative. "Okay. The average courting ritual goes like this: girl meets boy. Girl is wildly attracted to boy. Girl gets to know boy and falls in love. Bha'Kharian tradition for choosing its Queen is robbing you of this experience."

"Me?" he asked. "Or you?"

"Both of us."

"In the spirit of girl getting to know boy, I am told that I am quite a catch."

She'd heard her father tell Adina the same thing. "It's just that marriage is a big step, and pretty scary when one doesn't know one's intended from a rock."

He walked over to the French doors and looked out for several moments, then turned. A frown had replaced the good-natured expression on his face. "I do not believe anyone has ever compared me to a rock."

"That's just an expression. It means that I don't know you—"

"I understand the expression. But there is something I do not comprehend. In your training to be the Queen of Bha'Khar, it should have been explained that the period of engagement is the time to become acquainted."

"It was explained." Probably. But the step-by-step rules of courtship were still being violated. Father picks boy. Girl is engaged to boy. Girl meets boy and, after too brief a time, girl marries boy. And they live happily ever after? The odds were so against that.

She walked over to him and the breeze from the ocean cooled her face. Looking into his dark eyes, she asked, because she sincerely wanted to know how he felt, "What if it goes badly? What if you don't like me? What if I don't like you? What if we—?"

He touched a finger to her lips to silence her. "Do you always borrow trouble?"

"What if I do? Is that a deal-breaker?"

He laughed. "If I did not know better I would think you are deliberately trying to make me dislike you."

"Is it working?"

"I do not know."

"Do I need to try harder?"

"That depends on your purpose. I have not yet made up my mind about you. And you should not form an opinion about me, either."

"I'm not pre-judging—"

"I disagree. You came all this way to talk me out of this marriage, which means you have already closed your mind to the possibility that this arrangement could be a good thing."

She didn't see how it could be good, but that only proved his point. "What if I *have* formed an opinion already?"

He took a step closer. "Let go of your preconceived ideas." He touched his finger to her chin, nudging it up so their gazes locked. "Give me a chance to prove that I am indeed a good catch."

Beth didn't know whether to let out the breath she was holding or breathe deeply and overdose on his spicy, exciting scent, letting it invade and conquer her senses. A gleam stole into his eyes, a look that both excited and unnerved her. It was a purely masculine expression, full of male confidence in his power to get what he wanted.

There was little doubt in her mind that he would pull out all the stops in his mission to prove his worth, and seduction was right at the top of his list. While her romantic parts quivered with enthusiasm, her rational parts struggled to prevail.

"Malik, I have no doubt that you're a perfectly nice man. It was not my intention to insult you, and I apologize if I have."

"Your misgivings are understandable."

She wasn't sure if his easygoing manner made the situation better or worse. Although he was very attractive and charming, she had no reason to believe he was any different from the man who had discarded her in favor of his already chosen, politically correct wife. If anything, Malik was more powerful, and therefore more dangerous.

If it was up to her, she would tell this sheikh to take a flying leap. But it was Addie's choice. And, because her sister was choosing a time out, Beth was there to make sure she had it. In that spirit, she needed to dial down her opposition. "Thank you for your patience, Malik."

"You can repay me with patience of your own. Let us get to know each other. We will give it a chance and see what happens. Then if either of us has doubts we will choose an appropriate course of action."

In essence, he was asking for a truce. It would make things easier if he was a jerk and she could tell him what to do with his engagement.

On the other hand, if Malik decided this arrange-

ment didn't work for him either, and called off the
wedding, Addie would be off the hook and their
father couldn't hold it against her. So, truce it was.

She smiled. "How can I say no?"

Nine out of ten women would be overjoyed to be his
betrothed, yet Malik found himself with number ten.
Surprisingly, the idea did not rankle as he would
have thought. Obedience was a pleasing character-
istic in a woman, but after meeting Beth he realized
a fawning fiancée would be boring.

He was most curious about this lovely, stubborn
young woman who challenged him at every turn.
When she'd called him a powerful man, the edge in
her voice had warned him it was not a compliment.
Oddly enough, he was looking forward to this courtship, to the opportunity for changing her mind about
him and discovering the source of her misgivings
about marriage.

Malik walked into his dining room and touched
the control that lowered the chandelier illumination
to a romantic glow. Then he lit the candles on either
side of the fragrant flower arrangement gracing the
table. He had a bottle of the finest champagne cooling
in a silver bucket and crystal flutes waited expectantly, as did he.

Beth would be here any moment, and the dance
of learning about each other would continue.
Excitement hummed through him, and he realized he
had not experienced such a level of anticipation in
longer than he could remember. Of course, it had

been a long time since he had met such a fascinating woman. The last time it had happened he had been fooled. It was comforting and convenient to know there was no chance of repeating the same mistake with his betrothed.

He checked his appearance in the beveled gilt mirror in his suite's circular entryway. Every hair was in place, and he'd shaved a short while before—in case he kissed her, which he very much wanted to do. His silk shirt, open at the collar, and his dark pants evoked just the right informal tone, which was important, as he wished to put her at ease.

He heard a knock, so soft it would not have been audible had he not been standing near the door. Beth stood in the doorway, a vision of heaven in a high-necked, sleeveless white linen dress with a wide black belt that drew his attention to her small waist. It was a simple, elegant look, full of sophistication. The allure was in what he could *not* see as much as in what he could. Then he met her gaze and noticed the wariness in her large eyes—brown eyes, filled with flecks of gold.

He bowed slightly. "Good evening, Beth. Please come in."

"Thank you."

As she passed him, her subtle floral fragrance filled his head with visions that had nothing to do with gardens and everything to do with twisted sheets and bare flesh. Instead of entering, she stood and looked around. Of course she would be curious.

"Welcome to your new home," he said. "This is where we shall live after we are married."

"About the whole marriage thing—"

"Beth."

She turned to look at him. "What?"

"You promised to give it a chance," he reminded her.

"Promise may not be the right word. As I recall, my exact words were 'How can I say no?'"

He grinned. "Nevertheless, your response implied your agreement for us to get to know each other. In the spirit of that, I would request that for the duration of the evening you refrain from any negative references to a state of marriage between us."

"Is that a proclamation?"

"It is a heartfelt plea. And, under the circumstances, it is quite open-minded of me."

Her eyes sparkled with mischief, as he'd hoped they would. "So, Your Highness, can we talk about your humility?"

"Of course." He held out a hand and indicated the French doors off the living room. "Wait for me on the terrace and I will bring champagne."

"Is that an order?"

He did not miss the wary expression on her face, or the edge in her voice. Clearly she was expecting him to seduce her. It was a tempting thought, but that was not his plan. Not yet. No, tonight was all about charming her. There was a full moon, a warm breeze, and the fragrance of jasmine mixed with the scent of the sea. Mother Nature would wrap them in romance.

"Not an order. A suggestion. I simply thought you would enjoy the view and the fresh air."

"I see." Without further protest or a backward glance she walked through the living room and onto the terrace.

Malik opened the champagne and poured golden liquid into flutes, then carried them outside. He handed one to Beth.

"To what shall we drink?" he asked.

After thinking for a moment she said, "Loyalty."

That seemed an odd choice, but with his own painful lesson fresh in his mind he highly approved of her toast. "And honesty."

As they touched glasses, a musical tinkle sounded. Then Beth sipped from her flute as she gazed out over the sea. The moon's light created a silver path on the water, and the rhythmic cadence of the surf on the shore drifted up.

"Great view," she said.

"Yes." But his gaze was not on the sea. Malik was wondering if there was a more beautiful sight in the world than Beth by moonlight. And if his thoughts continued in that manner he was not at all certain he could resist her. "So, tell me more about yourself," he said, studying the long, graceful column of her neck revealed by her upswept hair.

The pulse at the base of her throat fluttered. "What do you want to know?"

"Tell me what happened to make you believe that love is not all it is cracked up to be."

"Oh, you don't really want to know about that."

"On the contrary. I believe it is at the heart of your resistance to marriage." Sipping from his glass, he studied her as she weighed his request.

"All right. There was a man. I met him when I was in college and there was an instant connection."

"You are in love with this man?" The idea produced a knot of resentment in him that seemed out of proportion to the amount of time he had known her, and that vexed him.

"Not anymore."

"But you were?"

"I thought I was."

"What happened?"

"He made me believe I was the only woman for him. Then he broke my heart when he married someone else."

The knot inside him eased somewhat and made rational thought easier. Then he realized something. "Surely you were aware that, as my betrothed, you are not permitted to give your heart to another man?"

"It was only my heart, Malik. To my everlasting shame, I couldn't help it. But at least I didn't compound my mistake by sleeping with him." She did not look away, but met his gaze directly.

They had just toasted honesty, and he had no reason to doubt her. "I believe you."

She sat on the low stucco wall surrounding the terrace and sighed. "I bet you're sorry you asked."

"Your candor is refreshing. The truth is not always easy, but it is preferable to pretense."

She was just sipping champagne and started to cough.

Malik sat next to her and took her glass. "Are you all right?"

She nodded and cleared her throat. "I swallowed wrong."

"I do not like it when that happens. I also do not like the thought of you and another man." That was the truth.

"As the relationship ended badly, there's no real harm done."

"I disagree."

"So you're going to hold it against me?" Was that hope in her voice? "If so, there's always the option of calling off the wedding. I can certainly understand if that's what you decide to do. Just say the word and I'll go back to America and—"

"On the contrary," he interrupted, noting that when she was nervous she was inclined to talk too much and too fast. "I believe a woman whose heart has known love once is more likely to look for it again."

"Even though I told you I don't want to be in love?"

"Even then."

"You're wrong." She shook her head and her full lips pulled tight. "I never want to feel that way again."

"Why?"

"If I'd never loved I never would have cried. And I promised myself it was the last time I would cry over a man."

He could understand the sentiment. He had made himself a similar promise about not being vulnerable to the charms of a woman. In his father's esteemed opinion Malik had shown poor judgment, and it could not happen again. Yet Malik's duty was to marry and produce an heir to succeed him on the throne. A love that burned him like wildfire would be unacceptable. And that was why marrying the woman chosen by his father was the solution. With Beth he could aspire to a fully contained warmth and respect.

Their shoulders brushed as they sat side by side and stared into the romantically dimmed light of the suite. Malik felt the soft skin of her forearm graze him and flames of desire heat up his blood.

"I feel compelled to point out that our betrothal is a good thing in light of your experience."

"How do you figure?"

"You can have all the benefits of marriage to the King of Bha'Khar without the messiness of dealing with love."

"So I can be like a man?" She met his gaze. The gleam of mischief mixed with challenge darkened her eyes.

The look was growing on him, but in no way prepared him for what came next. She smiled a smile that seemed to steal all the air from his lungs.

He picked up one of her small hands, then touched his lips to her knuckles. Satisfaction filled him to see the gleam in her eyes replaced by awareness. But, like her, he did not wish to be vulnerable to love. He was most pleased that they were in agreement, because his betrothed was quite a tempting combination of spirit and beauty. Theirs was a contract, a business arrangement, and that suited him well.

He brushed his thumb over the spot on her hand that he'd just kissed. "I cannot order or proclaim that you fall in love with me. But, little one, you will never be like a man." His voice dropped into the deeply seductive range. "And this man is extraordinarily grateful for that fact."

CHAPTER THREE

THE next morning Beth stood on her balcony with a cup of coffee in her hands while she looked out over the sea. Memories of last night clicked through her mind like a sensual slide show. Malik smiling his charming smile. Malik telling her he was glad she wasn't a man and kissing her hand. Her wanting to feel his lips pressed against her own, followed by disappointment when he didn't kiss her. Then the crushing guilt because she'd forgotten why she was there.

She leaned her hip on the low wall as the breeze caressed her face. Malik Hourani was not what she'd expected. He was kind, considerate and romantic. Damn him. If he didn't mess up soon, and do something to make her dislike him, the consequences couldn't be good. There was no way to put a positive spin on this charade. She was lying to Malik and her soul was doomed to the seventh level of hell. What was more, she deserved it.

She walked into the suite and picked up her cellphone, intending to call Addie and beg her sister to end this. Before she could put in the number, the phone attached to the landline rang.

She picked it up. "Hello?"

"Good morning."

There was no mistaking that deep velvet voice. "Malik. Good morning."

"I trust you slept well?"

"Never better," she lied, and realized the lies were getting easier, in spite of her resolution to tell as much of the truth as possible.

"I am glad to hear it. I have a surprise for you."

"What is it?" she asked.

"If I tell you it wouldn't be a surprise. But I will come for you in an hour."

"Where are we going?"

"You are attempting to trick me into revealing the surprise."

"Actually, I need to know what to wear."

"Dress casually."

Casually? That could mean anything, from jeans to a silk lounging outfit. "Casual as in sundress? Or casual as in pants?"

"Jeans," he said. "And that is all I will say."

The line went dead. Before she could stop it, excitement arced through her. In her life, surprises had been few, and usually bad. Her mother had walked out and her father wasn't the warm, fuzzy type. The man she'd loved had married someone else. But the pleasure in Malik's voice made her believe his surprise was something good, and she hurried to get ready.

In precisely an hour the Crown Prince showed up at her door, wearing jeans, a loose white cotton shirt and boots. He refused to say where they were going, but escorted her to the car he had waiting. A few minutes later they drove past white slat fencing that looked a lot like horse corrals. When the car stopped in front of a stable she had a very strong feeling that her good surprise was going to turn bad.

"Why are we here?" she asked, as he took her hand to help her from the back seat.

"I wish to show you the horse that my brother Kardahl purchased for you when he visited his wife's family. The mountain people raise some of the finest horses in the world."

Beth walked with him into the stable's shaded interior and realized the jig might very well be up. In finishing school, along with learning etiquette, how to throw elaborate dinner parties and protocol, Addie had become an accomplished horsewoman. Because all the royals were avid riders, it would be expected of the King's wife. On the other hand, Beth had never been on anything besides a carousel pony.

"I don't know what to say." After so many lies, it almost felt good to tell the truth.

"Come and meet the mare," he said, taking her hand. He led her to the stall where the animal stood waiting, her coat shiny black with splotches of white on her face. Addie would have been thrilled—would be thrilled—about this surprise. Beth—not so much. She was going to have to fly by the seat of her pants— so to speak. At the very least she needed to be polite.

"Thank you, Malik."

"You are most welcome."

Beth tried to look confident when she put her hand on the horse's neck. She knew enough that mare meant female. "Does she have a name?"

Malik smiled down at her, then chuckled when the horse nuzzled his shoulder. "As she is yours, you must choose what to call her."

"Jezebel." It was the first name that came to mind—from one shameless woman to another. At his questioning look, she shrugged. "I like the sound of it."

"Then Jezebel it is. I will have two horses saddled and we can ride—"

"No."

He frowned. "I do not understand. I was under the impression that my betrothed enjoyed riding."

"She does." On top of everything else, Beth realized she was talking in the third person, but technically it was the truth. Addie loved riding.

"Then I'm at a loss."

"It's just that I'm a little tired—"

"But you slept well."

And yet again her words came back to bite her. Oh, what a tangled web we weave...

"I did. But I lost count of how many time zones I crossed traveling here. I guess I'm still getting used to the difference. Jet-lagged."

"Another time, then. I should have waited, but I was anxious to give you this gift."

"I'm definitely surprised," she said, feeling like slime. "It's very thoughtful of you." Again, that was the truth. And, stretching it a bit, she said, "But I have to confess it's been a long time since I've been on a horse. I'm probably pretty rusty."

"Then we must make it a priority when you are sufficiently acclimated and well rested."

And by that time, if Beth hadn't alienated all the gods, Addie would have gotten her out of this situation.

"I'll look forward to that." She gave Jezebel one last pat on the neck, then walked out of the stables. Standing on the bottom rung of the fence, she rested her arms on the top and stared at the mountains in the distance.

Bha'Khar had a beauty all its own, and the air here seemed full of romance. While Malik would be nice to look at over breakfast every morning, there was more at stake than an unpleasant view. Beth had been watching her sister's back for as long as she could remember, and she couldn't stop now. Unless she could somehow convince Malik that this tradition was wrong there was every chance that Addie would be disowned. In Beth's view that would be preferable to Addie marrying and falling for him, because he would probably play by the rules of powerful men and break her heart with his infidelity.

Malik stood beside her, close enough that she could feel the heat of his skin. "You are looking most pensive about something. Would I be wrong to assume it is about our betrothal?"

"You would not."

"Tell me what you are thinking."

She sighed. "It just seems wrong to map out a person's life and rob them of free will."

"That is one point of view. Mine is that traditions are reassuring. And the custom of royal betrothal is even more reassuring than most. If you truly object to the marriage, you have only to say so."

"If only it were that simple," she said softly.

Her father would be furious. She and Addie had grown up under their father's thumb, learning to please him and trying to earn a rare word of praise in the battle to win his love. But Beth had realized early on that rebellion garnered his attention as following the rules did not. Finally she had come to the conclusion that he would never love her. Addie would become a queen, but she, Beth, was nothing special. So she'd followed her heart and become a teacher. When he had disowned her for choosing career over waiting for marriage, as he'd ordered, she hadn't expected it to hurt so much.

She'd always said, What's he going to do? Not care about me? But when he had indeed stopped caring about her, the pain of being cut off had been far worse than she'd realized. So Beth understood Addie's hesitation to stand up to him about the marriage. When her sister had begged Beth to fill in and give Addie a little time to see if she'd met "the one", time to find out if he was worth the price she would have to pay, Beth had agreed. Because she knew how hard it was to lose the only family you had.

Malik leaned his shoulder against the fence and stared down at her. "I do not know what is troubling you, but it is my wish that in time you will feel comfortable confiding in me."

"I appreciate the offer." He had no idea how tempted she was to do just that. If it were only about her, she'd confess in a heartbeat. But the truth wasn't hers to tell, and it could deeply hurt her sister. "Thank you, Malik."

"Something else I wish to point out is that there are worse things than having a map of one's life. Having things in perfect order is not a negative."

"Oh?" She met his gaze. "This from the man who likes surprises?"

"There can be surprises even in the context of a well-ordered life," he defended.

"So you like surprises as long as you're in control?" she observed.

"You say this as if it is a bad thing."

"Isn't it?"

"No." The sparkle in his eyes hinted at unexpected wonders, and her heart skipped twice before a deep breath steadied her.

"How's that working for you?"

The sparkle disappeared for just a second before he answered. "It works well. And, while we are on the subject, are there any surprises that you wish me to provide for you?"

"I don't know if it's a surprise, exactly."

"What is it you wish?"

It was the other reason she'd agreed to come here. "I'd like to find my mother."

"Even though she has not been a part of your life for many years?" he questioned.

So he knew about that. "Probably because of it. I just need to talk to her."

"Then I will arrange it," he said, without a moment's hesitation.

"Just like that?"

"Indeed."

"Thank you. I'm very grateful."

The mischievous twinkle reappeared in his eyes as his white teeth flashed in a heart-melting grin. "Might your gratitude include a kiss?"

It might, and all he had to do was stand there looking like sin for the taking. Her lips tingled with the temptation he offered. Jumping off the fence, she turned away and started to walk.

"I don't think so."

He followed. "Have I offended you?"

If only. "No."

"But I have made you uncomfortable?"

Oh, yeah. "Not really."

He wrapped his fingers around her upper arm to stop her, then turned her to face him. "Tell me the truth."

"I am not offended."

"Good." His smoldering gaze was like a magnet, refusing to release her. "Because there is something you must know."

"What?" she whispered.

"I *will* kiss you. And soon."

"Oh?" The single syllable was almost a squeak.

"When it happens, I wish it to mean something."

It would mean that she was going straight to hell. Do not pass go. Do not collect wings and halo. She was going to lose her soul.

"When it happens," he continued, "it will be because you cannot get me out of your mind. When our lips finally touch, you will feel it everywhere. The meeting of our mouths will be so sweet and deep and passionate that you will never want it to end."

Beth was speechless. And breathless. The intensity in his eyes, along with his words, removed any doubt that he meant what he said. When it happened, she wasn't sure she would be able to resist him. And that was a big problem, because he was romancing an imposter.

She was finding a lot to like about Malik, and lying to him was becoming harder and harder to defend. Agreeing to the ruse had been easier before she'd met him. She knew how it felt to be lied to, and as far as she could tell Malik didn't deserve it.

She had to talk to Addie.

With a cup of tea delivered by the palace staff in one hand and her cellphone in the other, Beth sank into the couch in her suite. She set the cup and saucer on the coffee table, then flipped open the phone and pressed commands until she got to her world clock and checked the time in Los Angeles.

"Too bad, Addie. We've got a crisis and it's worth losing sleep over." She hit speed dial and waited for the ring, then heard an answer.

"Hello?" Addie's sleepy voice came through loud and clear.

"Hi, Ad. It's me."

"Beth." All traces of drowsiness in her voice were gone. "Are you all right?"

"Physically, I'm fine. Everything else—not so much."

"What's wrong?"

"I have to tell Malik the truth—that I'm not you."

There was a silence on the other end of the line that had nothing to do with the distance delay. Beth could almost hear her sister thinking that over.

"What's going on?" Addie finally asked. "Is he suspicious?"

Beth grabbed a turquoise throw pillow and clutched it to her chest. "If he wasn't before, he probably is now. He gave me—you—a horse, and wanted to ride with me."

"Oh, my."

"No kidding, *oh, my.* You know how I feel about horses."

"What did you do?"

"I pretended to be tired from the trip and the time change." She was getting awfully good at pretending, and it wasn't something she was particularly proud of.

"Did he believe you?"

"I think so. I'm not sure." She plucked at the nubby pillow material. "I almost told him the truth."

"You can't, Beth."

Her stomach clenched. "I hate this. He seems like a really nice man, Addie. Romantic. Handsome. Kind. He's going to help me find our mother."

"Are you sure you want to confront her?" Addie asked.

"She walked out on us when we were just little girls without a word of explanation. She left us with a cold, unemotional man who flaunted his affairs, shipped us off to boarding school and tried to control our lives. You bet I want an explanation. I think she's selfish and shallow and I want to tell her so to her face." She took a deep breath to push out the knot pulling tight in her chest.

"Father means well," her sister defended. "In his own way he loves us."

"He loves *you*."

There was a deep sigh from the other end of the line. "I owe you so much, Bethie. You always took care of me and stood up for me. What would I do without you?"

Beth squirmed on the soft sofa, her backside remembering the blows. "You're my sister. I love you."

"I know. And I feel awful asking you to pretend just a little longer."

"You're going to like Malik a lot, Addie."

Beth wished he were an ogre. Then Addie couldn't marry him and their father would just have to get over it. But the Crown Prince's charm and wit made this whole situation more difficult.

"I need more time."

"Why?"

"I'm getting to know Tony. I think he could be special. I've never been in love, and I want to know what it feels like."

"It's not all it's cracked up to be," Beth said, remembering her conversation with Malik. He felt the same way, and they'd sort of bonded over their mutual aversion to more tender emotions. How inconvenient was that?

"If you could just give me a little longer."

"The rest of your life wouldn't be long enough to be sure. You're always going to wonder."

Like Beth wondered how in the world she could have been so stupid as to fall for a guy who thought he was entitled to a wife and a mistress because his political influence put him above regular people. Like she wondered if Malik thought he was entitled to step on whoever got in his way.

"If only the Crown Prince hadn't sent for me so suddenly," Addie said. "Everything was going along so nicely, and then he decided he wanted to act on the betrothal."

"The King is retiring soon and Malik will take over the throne. It's expected that he will be married and settled by his coronation," Beth explained. "I know. His timing couldn't be worse." Beth figured it couldn't hurt to try one more time. "Just tell Father you can't go through with this arranged marriage."

"I need to see if Tony is worth possibly losing my father," Addie pleaded.

"You're missing the point. Do it for *you*, not for a man. Stand up to him, Addie."

"I'm not as strong as you are, Bethie. I know Father can be overbearing, and he doesn't say what's in his heart. But I know he cares."

"If you weren't the firstborn—"

"By two minutes," Addie reminded her.

"It could be two seconds. The timing doesn't matter. You beat me out of the womb. Therefore you're the oldest and the one he promised to the Crown Prince. He could never tell us apart, but I guess he didn't have to, since he barely acknowledged I was alive."

"He's a flawed man, I grant you. But he's our father. I've already lost one parent and I'm not ready to say the words that could cost me the only one I have left. I need a little more time to work up the courage."

Beth closed her eyes. "All right. I won't say anything to Malik. For now."

"Thank you, Beth."

"Don't mention it. I'll do my best to be you until you get here."

When Beth had agreed to the deception she'd convinced herself it was the wrong thing for the right reason. That was getting more difficult to believe. She despised deceiving Malik, and she suspected the depth of her despicableness was in direct proportion to her growing attraction to him.

This fascination was completely unforeseen, since she hadn't expected to like him at all. Still, powerful men didn't necessarily show their true selves right away. Time would tell about Malik, and she hoped her sister showed up soon so Beth could hand off the problem.

Before her growing feelings became a bigger problem.

CHAPTER FOUR

"SURELY you have better things to do?" Beth stood beside the waiting town car beneath the palace portico.

At lunch the King and Queen had been charmed by their daughter-in-law-to-be, and had suggested that Malik show her around. Beth had said all the right things, but he had seen the hesitation in her eyes. He had felt a deliberate distance between them ever since his declaration several days before that he wished to kiss her. The more time he spent with her, the more acute was his impatience to make it so. The tension he felt in her now could be caused by his words, and that thought filled him with a great deal of satisfaction. It pleased him that his nearness could affect her. That meant he was not alone in his attraction.

He *did* have important things to do. After all, he was the Crown Prince of Bha'Khar, who would soon become King. But when his father, the current King, made a suggestion, Malik had learned the wisdom of heeding it.

"Better things to do than what?" he asked.

"Showing me around."

"You are my betrothed. It is my duty to introduce you to life in Bha'Khar in general and the experiences of the royal family in particular," he said, opening the car door.

She slid inside and brushed her shoulder against the opposite door, as far away from him as she could possibly get. "The royal family is very nice. I liked your parents and your brother and his wife a lot. But it seems to me that although you could have staffed out the palace tour, you didn't. And someone not as busy as you are *could* show me whatever it is I'm going to see now."

"I wish to be with you," he informed her.

Her uncertain gaze locked with his. "You were just with me. When you showed me the palace. I was pretty impressed by all those cars, although I lost count of the number of Rolls Royces, Bentleys and Ferraris."

"It is not the number that is important," he pointed out, recalling her amazement when he had shown her the palace garage. "But the fact that, should you wish it, there would be a vehicle at your disposal."

"Assuming I could locate them again."

"I would be happy to show you the way."

She shook her head. "Not necessary."

So she was continuing her attempt to keep him at arm's length. He had been told by more than one person that he was contrary and his reaction to Beth proved their point. The more she tried to push him away, the more he was determined not to let her.

"Did you not enjoy seeing where you will live?"

"I enjoyed it very much. But, just in case you're in the mood to surprise me again, instead of a horse I could use a GPS unit to plot my route. It's probably more efficient and accurate than a trail of bread-crumbs to find my way."

"You will get used to the palace."

"Better yet," she said, tapping her lip, "maybe some kind of transmitter or tracking device, so I could be located in the event that I don't show up when expected. Or a sign around my neck saying 'If lost, return to…'"

He laughed as the car moved smoothly past the palace gates and through the city. The sun reflected off the beige and pink stucco buildings with their white rock and red-tiled roofs as heat mercilessly baked the desert. After all, it was summer, but the interior of the car was cool. So far Beth had not said a negative word about his country, unlike her opinion regarding him. On that subject she had been most candid. Today he would show her that being the wife of the King of Bha'Khar was not all bad.

"The palace is not so big."

She shot him a skeptical look. "Yes, it *is* that big."

"There are bigger. I had the honor of visiting the Sultan of Brunei, whose palace is two hundred thousand square feet, including two hundred and fifty-seven bathrooms."

Her eyes grew wide. "So you had to share with the upstairs staff?"

"Hardly. My point is—"

"That your palace is a manageable space. Probably to you it is, because you grew up there and know your way around. But to me it's overwhelming. It's amazing, I'll grant you that—ballrooms, banquet rooms and meeting rooms—oh, my."

Malik had never given it much thought. He *had* grown up in the palace, and played with his brother there. It was his home, and had been in the royal family for several hundred years. He had explored all its nooks and alcoves, played hide-and-seek with Kardahl, and learned to successfully elude the governess, nanny and anyone else he did not wish to see. Unfortunately, it had not been large enough to elude the one woman whose agenda had included duplicity for the purpose of furthering her career.

He had grown up understanding his privileged position could be a magnet for personal gain, but he had not expected to encounter a schemer employed by the palace—under his own roof, so to speak. Because he had been taught to beware of con men, the lesson had been twice as bitter. He did not need another, and most definitely would not lose his heart again.

"So where are we going now?" she asked. "I've met your family, seen the palace—including enough cars to ensure transportation for a small country— and been to the stables. That doesn't include my airplane trip on the family jet. What else could there possibly be?" She glanced out the window and stared at the sea as they sped by. "About the only thing left is the royal yacht."

"Alas, you have guessed. Now it will no longer be a surprise."

"Is there more than one?"

"No. But it is big enough for the whole family."

A few minutes later the car was parked beside the yacht, and Malik was escorting Beth up the ramp to the deck. The captain, steward and cook greeted them, then discreetly disappeared as he showed her the bridge, dining room and several of the staterooms, with their mahogany walls and brass trim. Eyes wide, she followed him as he showed her all four decks of the two-hundred-sixty-foot yacht, including the spa and gym.

In the main salon, with its teak-trimmed walls, he asked the steward to bring them a cold drink. Malik felt the gentle sway of the craft and indicated she should sit on the beige leather circular sofa set in front of the square windows, overlooking the dock on one side, the sea on the other.

"So, tell me—what do you think?" he asked, sitting beside her. "I know you have an opinion."

"It's impressive." She looked through the large windows across from them. The surface of the sea gleamed like diamonds in the sun. "And what a way to escape."

Interesting way to phrase it. But before he could ask what she meant, they were interrupted.

The steward brought two glasses of sparkling water and set them on the stationary table. "Will there be anything else, Your Highness?"

"Thank you, Salleh. That will be all."

Beth sipped her water, then wrapped her hands around the cold glass. "I have to tell you I'm a little disappointed."

Her look was serious, but he was beginning to know the teasing gleam in her dark eyes. "Oh? How so?"

"It's all about guy toys. Cars, planes, yachts."

"You do not like these toys?"

"Don't get me wrong. I wouldn't turn down a cruise on the open sea. But I can't help thinking you forgot to show me the royal vault."

"I did not think it would interest you."

"It would if there are diamond tiaras, ruby necklaces and emerald rings inside. Where are the clothes, shoes and jewelry stashed? The things that make a woman's heart beat a little faster."

He suddenly realized that he did desire to make her heart beat faster—but not with jewels and clothes. He favored her good opinion because of this damned attraction that was more than he had expected to feel. The thought was disconcerting, as this arrangement was to be no more or less than business. It was never meant to be personal.

"If there is something that you desire, you need only voice your wish and I will make it come true."

She traced a finger through the moisture on the outside of her glass. "I wish you would call off the wedding."

So. They were back to square one, as the Americans would say. In one regard he was pleased that all the luxury he had shown her had not swayed her in her opinions. That spoke well of her character. Yet he had thought his impressive wealth would soften her attitude about becoming his wife.

"I do apologize." He had once felt as she did, resisting the tradition that allowed the King to choose his mate. But he had chosen poorly in love, which had changed his opinion about acquiescing to the decision of someone older and wiser than himself. He embraced the choice his father had made and the duty he would fulfill. There would be no emotional distractions. "That is the single request that I cannot grant you."

"I should probably warn you that I'll keep asking." She sighed. "I figured it couldn't hurt to try."

Hurt. A single word that made him wonder. It occurred to him that Beth had possessed royal approval from birth. She had the education and training required of the future Queen of Bha'Khar, yet she was still resistant to taking her rightful place. Was it possible that, despite her denial, she was still in love with the man who had cast her aside?

He took her glass and set it on the table, then took her cold hand between his own. He stared at her until her gaze met his. "I cannot help feeling that something more is bothering you."

"Nothing new," she said, glancing away.

"You are not still pining for the scoundrel who hurt you?"

A small smile curved her full lips. "I can truthfully say that I feel as if I dodged a bullet when he married someone else."

"You are certain?"

"Absolutely."

"As I said, I like surprises. As long as I am the one doing the surprising. I do not like being surprised. Now is the time to tell me if there is anything I should know."

"You know everything in my past that you need to."

That he needed to? Disconcertingly, he felt the need to know *everything*.

Her words were what he wanted to hear, but the shadows that flitted through her eyes made him doubt. He'd been fooled by a woman once and had not liked the feeling. Worse, he had given his love to an imposter. It would not happen again. He would give Beth whatever her heart desired—except his own heart.

That was a weakness that he would not repeat.

Beth stood quietly next to Malik before his brother's wedding rehearsal, still unclear about why it was happening. The wedding. Not the rehearsal. Posing for photographers, the royal family was standing on a dais in the front of a small room where the ceremony would take place two days from now. Next door, the main ballroom was being readied for a reception that would be attended by dignitaries from around the world. Surrounded by family, Kardahl and Jessica stood holding hands as they gazed adoringly into each other's eyes. Jessica's grandparents and two aunts were on one side. The King and Queen were on the other, with her and Malik.

Kardahl kissed his bride and cameras clicked,

while flashes went off like precision-timed explosives. Beth was blinded by the light and her jaw ached from smiling. On top of that, she was still not clear what all this fuss was about. It felt like overkill since Malik's brother was *already* married to Jessica—by proxy, Beth had been told. So it *was* possible for Addie's betrothal to be worse. Her sister could already be married, without having said "I do."

That would make Beth the proxy imposter. But pretending by any other name was still pretending, and it would have been even more awkward if he'd already believed her to be his wife and had expected sex.

A shiver went through her, and it wasn't because she was cold. Just the opposite. A man who could make her quiver from head to toe just describing a kiss would be devastating in bed. Probably. Beth would never know, and the thought carried a surprising bite of disappointment.

Malik must have felt her movement, because he looked down and asked, "Are you all right?"

"Fine. Just a little disoriented."

"The photographers?" he guessed.

Okay, she thought, shrugging, it would be less complicated to blame it on that. If she was actually his betrothed, it would be good that she was attracted to him. As the emissary sent by her twin to talk him out of the contract—not so much.

He slid his arm around her waist and gave her a reassuring squeeze. "It is a staged photo opportunity and will be over soon. During the actual rehearsal the media will be removed. The palace photographer will record the event for personal family remembrance."

"I see."

And, as if he'd ordered it, the wedding coordinator directed the security staff to clear the room. Beth moved off to the side and leaned against one of the ornate pillars that marched in a dignified line on either side of the room. While she watched, everyone in the wedding party was assigned their place.

As best man, Malik stood beside his brother. Jessica had her two aunts as attendants, and they were directed where to walk and stand. Her grandparents would be escorted in, then the King and Queen. After that the bride made her rehearsal trip down the aisle between the seats. She stopped in front of Bha'Khar's Minister of Justice, who would be officiating at the state rite. The bride and groom had written vows they were saving for the ceremony, but words were all Kardahl saved. He pulled his wife into his arms and proceeded to kiss the living daylights out of her.

As Beth watched, she heard Malik's voice in her head: *When our lips finally touch, you will feel it everywhere. The meeting of our mouths will be so sweet and deep and passionate that you will never want it to end.* The words produced a thrill that trapped the breath in her chest and made her skin flush with warmth.

The next thing she knew, everyone was filing out on their way to the rehearsal dinner, waiting in one of the smaller banquet rooms.

Malik extended his arm in a courtly gesture that indicated he would escort her. "Shall we join the others?"

"In a minute."

He frowned down at her. "Are you certain nothing troubles you?"

So much troubled her she could hardly count the ways, and yet she couldn't say anything to him. She hadn't realized this ruse would require quite so much deceit. Talk about not thinking something through. Pretending to be Addie had seemed easy. But now Beth had to pretend to like her betrothed. The downside was that this part wasn't a pretense. She actually *did* like him.

And it wasn't the kind of fondness that said how-nice-he-could-have-been-my-brother-in-law. It was more the kind of liking where he made her heart beat too fast and she wanted to be in his arms. More and more she had to remind herself that he could be a powerful man, putting on a good act to make her fall for him. Not her—Addie, she reminded herself. Beth wasn't there to fall under his spell. But more and more she wasn't believing her own hype, and her feelings were getting in the way. If she couldn't get them under control the consequences of playing this role could be personally devastating.

"I'm fine. Just confused."

"You have only to ask and I will ease your confusion."

"Okay. Here's the thing. I thought that Kardahl and Jessica were already married."

"You are correct."

"Then why are they getting married again?"

"They are in love and wish for the world to see how happy they are when they speak their vows face to face."

"Why didn't they do that the first time?"

He slid his hands into the pockets of his charcoal-colored suit pants. The movement disrupted the perfect line of his jacket. "Their union was accomplished through a proxy arrangement."

"So I was told. I find it hard to believe that actually still happens in this day and age."

He nodded. "It is perfectly legal."

"You sound defensive."

"On the contrary."

She studied the expression on his face and knew there was something he wasn't saying. "What aren't you telling me?"

He stared at her for so long it didn't appear he would answer the question. Finally he sighed. "It is a long story."

She glanced at the doorway where everyone else had disappeared. "I think we have time. We're only missing cocktail hour."

"You are not going to let this go, are you?"

She shook her head. "That's not my plan, no."

"As you wish." He leaned against the pillar. "Jessica was betrothed to my brother before she was born, but her mother disappeared in the United States. She was located at a tumultuous time in my brother's life, and our father was insistent on the marriage. The emissary he dispatched to facilitate Jessica's visit to this country was overzealous in the pursuit of his duties."

"What did he do?"

Malik glanced away, then met her gaze. "The proxy was written in Bha'Kharian. He put the agreement in a stack of papers for Jessica's signature and misrepresented the document when she inquired."

"Because he was trying to impress the King?"

"Just so."

"I see."

This confirmed all her worst fears about the abuse of power. She'd heard it said that absolute power corrupted absolutely. It wasn't that she thought anyone in Malik's family was underhanded or dishonest, but her fears went back to powerful men playing by their own rules. Beth had learned her lesson in a humiliating and painful way. She was a quick learner and didn't need a refresher course. What a relief that Addie had made up her mind to call off the marriage contract.

Malik straightened and crooked a knuckle beneath Beth's chin, lifting it so she would meet his gaze. "I think you do not see at all."

"How's that?"

"Kardahl and Jessica are an example of everything that is right about those wiser than ourselves choosing a life partner for us."

"Tell me what's so right about anyone but the man and woman involved deciding who they should marry."

"They fell in love, and are very happy with the results of their matchmaking."

"They got lucky," she said.

Against the odds. But she'd seen for herself how happy Jessica and Kardahl appeared to be. And Beth was truly happy for them. As for wiser men—she had trouble putting her father in that category. The man was cold and distant and didn't have a clue what kind of man would suit Addie. Or Beth, for that matter. Maybe he didn't care. Maybe it was all about power—through his daughter.

Beth loved her sister more than anyone in the world, and would do anything to keep her from being hurt. She wanted Addie to find a love like Kardahl and Jessica had.

And wasn't it ironic that Beth was attracted to Malik? Part of her regretted the fact that she would never know if it could have blossomed into something deeper. The other part reminded her that he would rule Bha'Khar soon. He was a powerful man, and her worst nightmare.

CHAPTER FIVE

MALIK half-listened as his brother made a toast to his bride at the rehearsal dinner. The family and friends gathered for the occasion lifted their champagne glasses in response. Photographers snapped pictures while the press recorded every word. The details of the wedding would be splashed on televisions, newspapers and magazines the world over. At least it was a positive story. No one could mistake the deep and genuine emotion the couple felt for each other.

It was good to see his brother happy, so deeply in love and…content. Malik felt the heartening outcome of this arranged marriage boded well for his own betrothal. Since he would ascend the throne when he married Beth the celebration would be on an even grander scale. A bud of anticipation took root and grew inside him—something he would not have believed possible for what he considered no more than a business deal. The realization did not please him.

Glancing around the chandelier-lit, flower-adorned room, he realized he did not see his bride-to-be, and wondered where she had gone. After scanning every corner without success, he felt a growing impatience to find her.

He walked through the French doors and onto the terrace. Lights from inside illuminated the tile patio that gave way to sand and eliminated the shadows almost down to where small waves lapped the shore. A full moon kept darkness at bay, and showed him a lone, slender female standing on the beach.

"Beth," he whispered, eager to feel the warmth of her beside him, hear her laughter and see the sparkle of her eyes by moonlight.

The sand slowed his progress, and as he moved closer it didn't escape his notice that she had removed the silver high-heeled sandals that had turned her legs into endless temptation. Her clingy black satin dress, high-necked and sleeveless, showed just enough bare flesh to fuel a man's fantasies. His acute reaction to her had nothing to do with the fact that she was his chosen—and he was not particularly pleased that he felt the way he did. These softer feelings rendered a man vulnerable, and dependent on the female to whom he was attracted. He would not call it love. He would never call it love again. Love, he had learned, was a lie, and he refused to let it taint his relationship with the woman who would be his Queen.

"Here you are," he said, coming up behind her.

She turned and did not look happy to see him. "I needed some air."

"Oh?"

"The crush of people was getting to me."

The breeze from the ocean made the curls around her face dance against her skin, and Malik's hands ached to touch the strands. He slid his fingers into his pockets and stared at the silver track of moonlight on the water. "I understand."

"You do?"

He felt her surprise; she had expected dissent. "Yes. The royal family is subject to intense scrutiny. Our every move is documented and chronicled the world over. Stories about us sell newspapers and magazines. It is just a regrettable fact of our life."

"Let me make sure I'm getting this. You're admitting that there's a downside to life in the royal fast lane?"

"I am."

"Wow," she said, shaking her head.

"Why do you sound so surprised?"

"Because you've been doing the full court press—"

"Define full court press."

"You've been pulling out all the stops to sell me on this royal marriage. You've been singing the praises of the wise old men masquerading as match-makers. I'm kind of shocked that you'd admit there's a flaw in the system."

"I apologize if that is the impression I have given you. Nothing is perfect. Palace life, while pleasant for the most part, has its downside."

That was an understatement. In the palace business wing he had felt insulated from the prying eyes of the world, until a woman had insinuated herself into his life. He had been foolish and thick-headed enough to lower his guard, and he had learned a valuable lesson. No matter how safe things seemed, caution was advisable, even with the woman chosen by his own father.

"Is there anything else I should know about palace life?" she asked.

"Many things."

"Pick one."

He thought for a moment, and it did not take long to choose just one. "Withhold your trust."

"That's very cynical."

"I have reason to feel this way."

She swung the silver sandals dangling from her fingers as she faced him. "You don't seem like an unreasonable man, so I'm sure you do. And, don't look now, but what you just said supports my negative feelings about this marriage."

It was no doubt a flaw in his nature that the more she fought against marrying him, the more he looked forward to it.

"And so we are back to this." He shook his head but could not suppress a smile. "You are not keeping to our agreement."

"Not true," she retorted. "I'm here, aren't I?"

Indeed, she was. In all her fresh and charming beauty. But it was not her physical presence he questioned. "You take every opportunity to point out the unpleasant parts of life as a member of the royal family. To my way of thinking that violates the spirit of your promise to keep an open mind."

Yet, in spite of her inclination to do this, she stirred something inside him. It wasn't simply her beauty—there were many beautiful women in the world, and he had known a good number of them before committing to this betrothal. Her intelligence and humor were appealing qualities, but he'd met smart, funny females before. So what was it about this one that he found so enticing?

Perhaps it was the very thing he questioned her about: the fact that she resisted marriage to him at every turn. This could be because the one who had betrayed him had flattered and manipulated her way into his heart and he had not seen what she was doing. Beth, on the other hand, made no secret of her opinion. She was charmingly honest and refreshing. And her full lips, soft and alluring in the moonlight, were almost more than he could resist.

"My mind is open," she protested. "I'm simply taking every opportunity to debate the issue."

"Debate is all well and good. It is exhilarating. But it would be a disservice for me to not be honest about the drawbacks. And royal life does have them."

She thought about that for several moments. "Now that you mention it, I guess it must be difficult to maintain friendships in your position. People want something from you, and you never know whether they like you for yourself or what you can do for them."

Truer words were never spoken, he thought.

"More than the lifestyle restrictions, feigned interest for personal gain is by far the most difficult aspect of royal life."

"Does this have anything to do with what you told me about making a poor choice in love?" She studied his expression more closely. "Wow, I think I hit a bull's-eye."

She had indeed. The truth of her words tightened and twisted inside him, scraping his nerves raw and reigniting the anger he had thought was gone. "That is not something I wish to discuss."

"Are you still in love with her?"

"Absolutely not," he hotly denied.

"Hmm. Methinks he doth protest too much. Should I be jealous?" she asked.

"That is a decision you must make for yourself."

"Your wife would be justified in her jealousy if you married her, and yet continued to carry on with another woman after the wedding."

"I am insulted that you would suggest such a thing."

"Why? Men do it all the time. Especially powerful men who think basic rules of decency don't apply to them because they *are* powerful."

This was not the first time she had said such a thing. She questioned his principles, but he wondered if her queries sprang from a place where she still harbored deep emotion for the man who had broken her heart. The thought produced a stab of something that was common and distasteful and disturbingly like the jealousy they had just been discussing. He had already questioned her and she had denied any feelings. It was the truth as she knew it. He would tell the truth as well, and in time she would know the sincerity of it.

"She no longer matters to me," he said.

Except inasmuch as he would never forget or forgive being made a fool of.

"Then why haven't you kissed me?" Beth's eyes widened, as if she could not believe she had spoken the thought out loud.

"If you believe nothing else, believe this." He curved his fingers around her upper arms and brushed his thumbs over the soft flesh. The blood in his veins stirred and grew hot as he stared at her mouth, the beautiful tempting lips that had kept him awake nights. "Since the first time we met, I have thought of very little besides kissing you."

"B-but you haven't. Kissed me, I mean." The pulse at the base of her throat throbbed and her voice was breathy with desire.

Satisfaction poured through Malik when he realized that she was affected by his nearness. Words could be twisted, and were open to interpretation regarding sincerity. But he did not believe she could feign her body's response to him any more than he could pretend his own wasn't aching for her. He would not give his heart to any woman, but, with an impatience he had never known, he wanted *this* woman in his bed.

"I have not kissed you," he agreed, his voice harsh even to his own ears.

He bent his head and felt her breath touch his lips.

Their mouths were a whisper away, but if Beth had taught him anything it was that denial increased attraction. The more she challenged their betrothal, the more acutely he wanted her. But he wanted her to want him with the same intensity. When he finally kissed her, he wished her to crave it like her next breath.

"I will correct the oversight," he said. "Soon."

Beth rode beside Malik in the town car, and again he'd been mysterious about their destination. A man who liked surprises. That made her uneasy. She wondered what he would show her this time, and struggled to generate enthusiasm instead of feeling so crabby.

As if the wedding rehearsal and reception, complete with media frenzy, hadn't strained her emotional reserves enough, she'd held her breath on the beach, waiting for Malik to kiss her. Glancing over at him now, in the seat beside her, she sighed. She was still waiting, and the frustration had kept her awake long into the night. If only she'd been able to get the conversation out of her mind.

His brooding look when she'd questioned him about love had convinced her he still harbored deep feelings for a woman. Jealousy had trickled through her, followed by an intense reaction to give whoever had hurt him a piece of her mind. If that hadn't convinced her she was no longer an impartial place-holder for her sister then her profound disappointment at him not kissing her certainly did.

With every fiber of her being Beth had wanted—

no, *needed*—to feel his lips against her own. Yet he'd held back. She could have cheerfully choked him, and a few hours alone hadn't diminished the heat of the emotion.

When he'd arrived at her suite with an invitation to take a drive, she'd almost told him what he could do with it. Except she'd been too happy to see him. And that was bad. She had no right to be so happy about spending time in his company. She also had no choice.

So they'd been driving. And now the elegant car pulled to a stop in front of a small, square white stucco house with a flat roof and a tiny yard landscaped with rocks to complement the desert.

Beth looked at him. "Are we there yet?"

"We are."

The driver opened the door and Malik got out, then took her hand to assist her. She slid out and looked around. "Where is 'there'?"

"This is your mother's house. She is expecting you."

Her gaze snapped to his. "How did you—?"

"I have my ways. I am a powerful man." He grinned.

Beth turned and saw a woman about her own height standing in the open doorway, staring at her with a combination of expectation, hope and anxiety on her face. She was wearing a cream-colored, cap-sleeved, full-skirted cotton dress that came to mid-calf. Her silver-streaked dark hair was parted in the center and pulled into a knot at her nape.

Malik held out his arm. "Your mother is waiting."

Beth put her hand into the bend of his elbow, but her legs started to shake as they walked up the short sidewalk and stopped in the shade on the front porch.

The two women stared at each other for several moments, simply studying one another. Then her mother said, "Beth."

Tears burned Beth's eyes. This woman knew *her*. Almost instantly she'd known Beth for herself, and hadn't mistaken her for Addie. Then the years of abandonment flashed through her memory, and the heat of anger dried up her tears.

"Hello, Mother." There was an awkward moment when she saw the woman lift her arms for a hug, but Beth stood still, not moving into them.

"Please come in," her mother said, hurt flashing in her dark eyes as she stood aside to let them enter. "I am Sameera Farrah, Your Highness," she introduced herself.

He shook her hand. "It is a pleasure to meet my fiancée's mother."

Beth went cold as she met her mother's surprised gaze. This woman recognized her as Beth, and she knew which of the twins was betrothed to the Crown Prince. Beth shook her head, a small warning movement, and comprehension flashed in the other woman's eyes.

"May I offer you some refreshment?"

"Thank you, no. I cannot stay." He met Beth's gaze. "I simply wished to fulfill my promise and surprise you."

"Mission accomplished," Beth said with a shaky laugh.

"I will leave you now, so that you can talk privately. The car will return and wait to take you back to the palace."

What a sweet, thoughtful and nearly catastrophic gesture. Beth lifted her arms to hug him. "Thank you."

He pressed her close. "You are most welcome."

His gaze held hers for a long moment, then he was gone.

Beth savored the cool air against her hot cheeks as she glanced around the small room and noted the wood floor, white sofa and glass-topped coffee table. When she could no longer avoid it, she looked at her mother.

"Would you care for a cold drink?" She shook her head and Sameera held out her arm. "Then let us sit."

"Okay." Beth gratefully lowered herself to the soft cushions.

"I take it the Crown Prince is unaware that you are impersonating your twin sister?" Her mother sat to her right.

"Yes." It was weird, this sensation that there was nothing she could hide from this woman. And that begged the question. "How did you know I was me? Not Addie?"

Her mother reached out a shaky hand, then brushed a thumb across Beth's cheek and down her neck. "You have a small birthmark behind your ear. When you were first born, it was how I knew you from your sister. Before your personalities developed and made you distinct."

Beth touched her neck. She'd forgotten about it. "Is Father aware of this mark?"

"I brought it to his attention when you were first born."

"Apparently he forgot," she said wryly. "He never knows which of us is which. In fact the only attention I get from him is when he thinks I'm Addie. Otherwise he pretty much ignores me."

"You were not the first born. You were not the one who was promised to the future King of Bha'Khar."

"And you're not the least bit surprised by his behavior." Suddenly Beth knew her mother had known what would happen to her, and still she had simply walked away and let it happen. Years of resentment and loneliness and neglect came flooding back. Hurting over and over because no one had ever loved her. No one but Addie.

"How could you leave me with him?" She said it quietly, carefully, to keep her voice from cracking.

"You did not get my letters?" Shock, sadness, then resignation deepened the age lines in her mother's face.

"What letters? We didn't get any messages from you. You walked out on us."

Sadly, Sameera shook her head. "I wrote every day for months. Years."

"You wrote to us?" It was something she'd never considered.

"Obviously my letters were intercepted. I was afraid of that."

Her sigh was soul-deep. "If I were you, I would have doubts, too. But believe this—I love you, Beth.

And I love your sister. My girls, my twin daughters, are more important to me than anything in this world." Her mother folded her hands in her lap and said quietly, "I did not leave. Your father took you from me."

"I don't understand. Why?" She held her hands out in a helpless gesture. "Why would he do that?"

"Because I was going to leave him."

Shock didn't begin to describe Beth's feelings, and all she could say was, "Why?"

Sameera sighed, and her dark eyes took on a faraway, pained look. "It was after I had a visit from his mistress."

"What?"

"She told me that he had never been mine. That he'd simply married me because of my distant connections to the royal family. They had been lovers before he married me, and the affair had continued to that day."

"Oh, my—" Beth pressed a hand to her mouth, trying to absorb the information.

"I was shocked, but refused to believe what she said. Only after the information was confirmed did the humiliation set in. That was when I told him the marriage was over."

"And then?" Beth asked, but she knew what was coming.

"Your father was a rising star in the Bha'Kharian diplomatic service. He used his power and influence to take you away."

"To the United States?"

Her mother nodded. "He'd received an appointment and we were making plans for the move. I confronted him, and he simply took you and Addie and left without me."

"I can't believe he would do that."

"Can't you?" Her mother's look was wry.

"Okay, I can believe it. But why didn't you come after us? Why didn't you fight for us?"

"I tried. I followed, and tried to see you. But he kept me away. He has diplomatic immunity. He has connections. Bodyguards. Staff. He was able to insulate himself from everything. I couldn't break through. I waited and watched, but then I found out he had sent you away to school. No one would tell me where you were and I did not know how to find you. That's when I started sending the letters, hoping they would get to you somehow. I received only one response—a letter from you and one from your sister, saying that you did not wish to see or hear from me ever again."

Beth was stunned. "I didn't send that message. Neither did Addie. I swear."

Tears gathered in her mother's eyes, and when her mouth trembled, Beth desperately wanted to comfort her.

"It must have been Father. I know he's cold-hearted, but I had no idea he was a liar, too." She winced at her own words, unwilling to believe that she was at all like him, recent dishonest behavior to the contrary.

"I believe you." Sameera reached over and

squeezed her hands. "But you must believe that I always loved you and your sister with all my heart. I never stopped loving you and I never will."

"I should have known," Beth admitted. "But too many years of Father's indoctrination took a toll."

"If anyone understands this, it is I. As I understand that there is undoubtedly an explanation for the fact that you are impersonating your sister."

"There is."

And her mother had just reinforced the necessity of this pretense that was giving Addie the time and space she needed to end the engagement in her own way.

Beth thought it a sad irony that she and her mother shared the dubious distinction of being a cautionary tale on the perils of loving a powerful man. For the first time in her life she felt a measure of peace.

She took a deep breath. "When the Crown Prince decided it was time to activate the arranged marriage, Addie wanted to call it off. But she's reluctant to stand up to Father and risk being disowned."

"I wish I could say he would not do that, but I have lived through the trauma he is capable of causing."

"So have I." Beth filled her in on her own experience. How she'd confronted her father about her teaching ambitions, then felt his displeasure, followed by his rejection, when she had refused to abandon her career goals and wait for marriage, as he'd ordered.

Sameera moved close and put an arm around Beth's shoulders. "For what it is worth, I am proud of you for standing up to him. If anyone understands how difficult that is, it is me."

"That means a lot." Beth smiled. "Not only that, Addie met a man she really likes. She begged me to step in, just for a little while, so she can figure out how to handle Father."

"So the two of you have switched identities? And you have become acquainted with the Crown Prince?" Her mother's look was penetrating. "What is he like?"

"His Highness the hunk?" An instant visual flashed through her mind. "He's handsome—but you saw that for yourself." Beth felt her face flush. "He's kind and thoughtful. Funny. Smart."

"I would say your sister is not the only one who has met a man she really likes."

When her mother smiled a knowing smile, Beth protested. "No. Well, yes, I like him. But it's not what you think. I don't *like* him, like him. He's not my type. So it would be wrong to like him…like that," she finished lamely.

"And you plan to step aside when all is resolved?"

"Of course," she answered, without hesitation.

"Let me rephrase. Are you becoming too fond of this man? Will you be able to let him go without regret? Without hurting your heart?"

"Of course."

But this time there was little or no conviction in the words. In spite of the fact that her mother had just confirmed that her worst fears were justified, Beth was unable to deny her attraction to the most powerful man in Bha'Khar—the man who would be King.

For the first time she was grateful he hadn't kissed

her under the full moon last night. Love at first sight
was a long shot, and she'd survived that. But love at
first kiss was something else again. She had a bad
feeling that Malik might bring her to her knees, and
she didn't intend to let that happen ever again.

CHAPTER SIX

IT WAS a breathtakingly beautiful wedding.

Beth watched from her front row seat as Kardahl vowed that family was the most important thing and Jessica was now his family. In front of dignitaries from around the world, their friends and, most important of all, their families, the two pledged to love and respect each other forever. She noticed that the word "obey" was left out of the official Bha'Kharian vows, as well as the informal ones they'd written to each other.

Beth pretended to brush her fingers over her cheek as she discreetly wiped away the tears that just wouldn't be suppressed. Under a star-jasmine-covered arbor, the bride and groom looked out over a room transformed from four walls and a ceiling into a magical garden, with red roses and small white lights strung through lush plants.

Kardahl was handsome in his tuxedo, with traditional neckwear instead of a bowtie. And Jessica looked every inch his perfect bride, a princess in a cream-colored dress with a long-sleeved bolero jacket, a tied satin bow at the waist and a full skirt. It was every little girl's fantasy come true, and Beth was no exception. She shed a tear or two for her own dream, that wouldn't come true because she had no illusions about finding love.

Speaking of forbidden love, she had difficulty taking her eyes off Malik, who stood beside his brother. He was also in a dark suit, and so extraordinarily handsome he took her breath away. Something about the formalwear made his dark eyes look darker and his sensuous mouth more seductive. The slight flare in his nostrils hinted at a depth of passion she could only guess would sweep a girl off her feet and make her love every second.

Beth's heart skipped like a stone over water, then pounded frantically as she lifted a hand to her bodice and drew air deeply into her lungs. Her own royal blue dress had been a surprise from Malik, sent from a Paris designer and fitted right here in the palace. The long sleeves, high neck and floor-length skirt clung to her body like a second skin. Sapphire teardrop earrings dangled from her earlobes and the matching tiara held her upswept hair in place. Jewelry from the Queen's collection had been loaned to her for the occasion, proving that Malik had told the truth about life with the royals having an upside.

She actually felt like a princess—and, worse, she liked it. That was probably normal, but it made her feel like she was selling out her soul.

When the ceremony was over, Malik stopped

beside her and offered his arm to escort her to the enormous banquet room for the reception. She was getting used to his courtly gestures. They were doing a lot to soften her up, and the heat in his eyes when he looked at her only speeded up the melting process. She put her hand in the bend of his elbow, but closed her fingers into a fist, refusing to relax into the intimacy.

Malik didn't seem to notice as he smiled and nodded to the Prime Minister of Britain and the Chancellor of Germany. The United States' Secretary of State was also in attendance. To her relief, her father had sent his regrets because of work. But the guest list was like a *Who's Who* of world power, and Beth was both grateful for Malik's presence beside her and so nervous she felt like throwing up. The woman he married would have to get used to this.

When they entered the other room, Beth stopped him. "I need to freshen my make-up."

"I will wait for you."

She shook her head. "That's not necessary. I'm sure you have to mingle."

"As do you," he pointed out. "I wish to introduce you to the world as my bride-to-be."

"No rest for the wicked," she mumbled.

"Do not worry. You have been trained, and will become accustomed to this part of royal duty."

"The real thing is a lot different from the class-room," she pointed out.

"I will be by your side every moment."

"Then it's important to look my best." She waved him off. "Go. I'll find you."

He took her hand and curved her fingers around his own, then touched his lips to her knuckles. "I will count the seconds until you are beside me again."

She wanted to ask how that line was working for him. But her throat was too dry because the words were firing on all cylinders for her.

The ladies' lounge had individual mirrored vanities, with tufted brocade-covered stools in front of them. The floor was marble, where it wasn't thick carpet. Gold fixtures adorned the cream-colored sinks, and the recessed lighting would flatter complexions of all ages. Beth found Jessica sitting at one of the vanities, struggling with her headpiece and veil.

"Boy, am I glad to see you."

"Where's your entourage?" Beth asked, meeting the bride's distressed gaze in the mirror.

"I sent them into the reception. I thought I could handle this by myself, but it's more complicated than I expected." She pointed to where the yards of tulle were fastened. "It's supposed to detach from the tiara and leave my hair intact. Can you help me?"

"I'll see what I can do."

Standing over the other woman, Beth could see the problem and easily took care of it. The intricate feminine knot of hair was left undisturbed except for light brown tendrils around Jessica's face. "There," Beth said, draping the veil on the satin-covered chaise behind them.

"You're a lifesaver."

Beth pulled a stool over and sat beside the bride

while she touched up her blush and lipstick. "That's a waste of time, because you look perfect."

"Oh, please." But Jess's hazel eyes sparkled when she smiled. "Not true, but thanks for saying it. I don't think I've ever looked better, but 'perfect' is setting the bar a little too high."

"You're wrong," she answered simply. "The ceremony was perfect, too."

"I'll go along with that. I wish I could rewind and go through it over and over, and take it all in without the nerves. It felt surreal, like a dream. In fact it *was* my dream, and it came true."

"So you're happy?" Beth asked.

Jess sighed. "I had no idea it was possible to be this happy."

Beth realized this woman understood what it was like to love a powerful man. She seemed happy. Or was she simply toeing the official royal family line? Had she missed her calling as an actress? Or was she sincerely as ecstatic as she appeared?

"So tell me what it was like when you first met Kardahl."

Jess sighed. "It wasn't pretty."

"Oh?" Maybe she was getting somewhere. Beth had expected a fairytale, but the story hadn't started out with "once upon a time."

"I hadn't even deplaned when Kardahl informed me that we were already married by proxy."

"Malik told me what happened. How did you feel?"

"I'd only just found out about my mother's past, and was here to see if there was a chance I had a family. So it was pretty shocking to discover I had a husband." She shook her head as she remembered. "You can imagine how I felt."

"Not really."

"Just picture the worst moment in your life and multiply it by a hundred. I wanted someone punished for the snag in paperwork that had made me his wife. I wanted nothing to do with love. You could say I was a reluctant bride."

"What changed your mind?" Beth asked.

"In a word: Kardahl."

"Did he pressure you and make a case for how wonderful life would be as a royal?"

Jess shook her head. "Just the opposite. He said if I wasn't happy we would get an annulment as long as the union wasn't consummated."

"Obviously the annulment didn't happen, and I don't think it's too big a leap to assume you've consummated the marriage at least once?"

"Oh, yeah." She blushed prettily. "In fact, we just told the King and Queen that we're expecting a baby. I just found out I'm pregnant."

Emotions swept through Beth—happiness for the other woman, and envy at her good fortune. She leaned over for a quick hug. "Congratulations. Does Malik know?"

"Probably by now." Jess folded her hands and rested them on the satin skirt. "I grew up in a state home after my mother died. Girls like me don't grow up to become a princess, but Kardahl loves me anyway. And I love him. If he were poor as dirt I would still love him, because even if there was no connection to a royal family he would still treat me like a princess. That's the kind of man he is."

"So I guess I don't even have to ask if you were okay with being betrothed to a man you'd never met?"

"Kardahl believes it's not about the tradition of betrothal. It was fate that brought us each other. We were meant to be together."

"It's a very romantic notion," Beth agreed.

The other woman must have heard the wistful note in her voice. "You're worried about you and Malik?"

"Something like that."

Jess reached over and took her hand. "I understand. And the only advice I can give is to relax and go with it."

"I'll try." Beth stood. "You need to go back in there and celebrate."

Jess's eyes filled with happy tears. "And I have so much to be happy about I almost feel guilty."

Jessica's story, even with its positive outcome, did nothing to diminish Beth's misgivings about powerful men living by their own rules. Malik was charming, attentive, handsome and sexy. He was out in that ballroom right now, rubbing shoulders with some of the most powerful men in the world. It was his job.

She was in the ladies' lounge alone, thinking about him and missing him, she realized. But the woman who married him would get used to being alone, because power was only one of his mistresses.

The thought distressed her, but there was something that bothered her even more. She already cared enough to *be* distressed.

Beth had never been to a more perfect wedding reception—exquisite food, red and white roses signifying love's passion and purity, tables with their lovely and delicate gold place-settings looking magnificent. Now, the chandeliers that moments ago had dripped shimmering golden light were dimmed for dancing in the center of the room.

There was no reason to think that whoever Malik married wouldn't have an even more beautiful wedding. But it was still just one day. No matter how glorious the festivities, the next day his bride would be legally bound to the man who would be the King of Bha'Khar. Would he be a good husband? Would he cherish and be faithful to his wife? Or would he use his prominent position to have any woman he wanted?

As she was the woman currently in his arms, dancing, it wasn't a good time to be asking herself that. It was an even worse time to realize that while looking into his handsome face all she could think about was how he had such wonderful hair she wanted to see how it would feel to run her fingers through it.

"You are a graceful dancer," he said, pulling her just a bit closer to him.

"Thank you. So are you."

"Did you learn in finishing school?"

His warm fingers flattened against the bare flesh of her back and produced a shiver of major proportions. Her breasts snuggled against his muscular chest turned her fantasies to physical activities other than dancing. In fact they were the kind of activities that usually didn't involve standing upright at all.

"Yes," she said, her voice too low, too breathless. "We all had to learn."

"But it was an all-girls school," he said.

"We managed to memorize the steps, and there was an all-boys school nearby. We practiced with them at cotillions."

"Ah," he said, nodding. "Practice makes perfect."

The gleam in his eyes and his slow, sexy smile only succeeded in throwing her more off balance.

"So, what did you think of the wedding?" she asked, searching for a safe topic of conversation.

"I think it is not the ceremony that matters so much as the fact that my brother is happy and most content."

"But will he still love her tomorrow?" she asked.

His dark eyebrows drew together. "You are the most skeptical young woman I have ever met."

"Have you known many young women?"

"Of course."

"Anyone special?"

"No one of consequence."

"And not skeptical?"

"Not so much as you," he said, the teasing look back in his eyes. "My brother and his wife are deeply in love, and there is no doubt in my mind it is a union that will endure a lifetime."

"Is that wishful thinking? Or are you a romantic?"

Not likely. To men like him power was the aphrodi-siac, not romance.

"I know my brother well, and I have never seen him as happy as he is now. He spoke vows in front of the world and his love for his betrothed will be chronicled for all time in Bha'Kharian history." His gaze caught hers as he held her securely in his arms. "But right now, this moment, is the highlight of today's festivities."

"Dancing?" Her heart speeded up, like a small but painful hammer inside her chest. "So you like to dance?"

"Not especially."

"Then why is this your favorite part?"

He smiled. "Your naïveté is so unexpected, and therefore so completely delightful."

She couldn't decide whether she'd been compli-mented or insulted. "I thought I was the most skep-tical woman on the planet?"

"You are that, too. I am enjoying the many facets that make up the woman I will marry."

She blinked and lowered her gaze. "But if you're not into dancing, can one assume that this is a dis-traction from the affairs of state that are so much a part of this public occasion?"

"One can assume that. You are definitely a distrac-tion—a most welcome and charming one."

He was a distraction, too. Every time she got near him she was unsettled, disconcerted, confused and flustered by his keen intelligence, his magnetism and sense of humor. She was sidetracked, and kept forgetting that she was just a placeholder, just filling in for the only other person on the planet who looked like her. She was saving her sister from this man. She had no business being susceptible to him herself.

The problem was, he thought she *was* his betrothed, and to impress her he'd turned up the charisma full-blast. It was so working. There was a time to stand and fight, and there was a time to cut and run. As she saw the intensity gather and darken in his eyes, running held more—and less—appeal.

"Excuse me. I think I need some air," she said, freeing her hand from his. "And you should mingle."

Before he could respond, she turned and slipped through the crush of couples dancing, keeping her eyes on her goal—the French doors that led onto the patio. She slipped outside and let out a long cleansing breath. Inside the palace was fantasyland; outside was magic, she realized. The kind of magic that only Mother Nature could produce.

The air was warm, and scented with jasmine and the mysterious fragrance of the sea. The moon spread a path of silver light on the placid water.

Beth wandered over to the low wall that looked out on the water and let the breeze cool her hot cheeks. Behind her, she heard the door open and strains of music escape before it was closed again. She sighed, because she knew who was there. Her luck wasn't good enough that he could just let her go without comment. Out of the frying pan, into the fire.

"Have I offended you?" he asked.

She shook her head. "No."

"I am aware that the responsibilities of my betrothed can be daunting. But do not forget that experience and confidence come with time. You will have a staff, and advisers to assist you with every state duty."

He thought she was having second thoughts about being the wife of the King. And he'd followed to reassure her. How incredibly sweet was that? If only her distress was so simple.

"I'm fine, Malik. I just needed some alone time." It seemed the more she tried to keep her distance, the more he was there.

"Time to question the role you will assume when we are married?"

She met his gaze, then wished she hadn't. He was pretty spectacular in ordinary settings, but by moonlight he was irresistible. "Who in their right mind wouldn't question it?"

He nodded. "I see your point. However, I believe I have been remiss."

"What? How?"

"You have made your position on love clear, and I understand and agree. However, that does not mean that we cannot find mutual respect and pleasure in each other's company."

"That doesn't explain how you've been negligent."

"There are responsibilities that go along with being Queen. But there are also rewards. I have been inattentive to your needs."

"No." She shook her head. He'd been unfailingly attentive.

"I disagree. Often a man has no opportunity to rectify a mistake, but thankfully this is not one of those times." He moved closer, a whisper away. "I did not kiss you when I had the opportunity."

Oh, God. She'd thought she'd caught a break the other night. "It's okay," she answered, taking a step back.

"It is not okay."

"But you said the first kiss should mean something. I don't see what—"

"It means that we are beginning a new chapter in our courtship. It means that we will take a first step in the process of getting to know each other physically, come to an understanding, create a spark on which to start a fire. That from this moment on we will build a foundation for a life together that is made up not of something as fragile and unreliable as love, but of mutual warm regard, respect and trust."

"About all of that—"

She lost the thread of her thoughts when he looked at her with one long, intense, measuring glance, then reached a hand out and tucked a strand of her hair behind her ear. He curved his fingers behind her neck and caressed the column of her throat with his thumb, mesmerizing her with the seductive motion. Then he bent and touched his lips to a spot just beneath her ear, a place that seemed to hold the key to her willpower and rational thought because suddenly both vanished.

"You are so beautiful, my sweet," he whispered against her skin.

Then he cupped her face in both hands, tilted her mouth and stared for a long moment before lowering his lips to hers. The soft touch was a banquet for her senses, a feast of the flesh. Hers felt warm, as if she stood too close to a fire. In fact, she was right in the middle, and it was getting hotter by the second as he wrapped her in his arms and crushed her breasts against his chest.

He kissed her again and again, his breathing growing harsh when a small moan slid from her throat. She opened her mouth to him and he dipped his tongue inside, taking without hesitation what she couldn't help offering. But the act of mimicking lovemaking did nothing to relieve the pressure building inside her and everything to fuel it.

When he pulled back they were both breathing hard. He rested his forehead against hers as he sucked in air. "Tell me the truth. Tell me, if you dare, that this did not mean something."

Oh, how she wanted to, but it would be a lie. And she'd promised herself she would tell the truth when at all possible.

"I can't," she whispered.

In fact, it meant so much more than he could possibly know. It meant more than the fact that he was charming her. It meant more than trying to talk him out of the arranged marriage.

It meant that Beth was responding to him in a very basic, very primal, very female way. This kiss put the truth right out there, and she couldn't run from it any longer. She wasn't pretending to be attracted to the man her sister was supposed to marry.

She was way beyond attraction and in danger of becoming an emotional disaster area, by again falling for the wrong man.

CHAPTER SEVEN

MALIK looked around the ballroom. He had not seen Beth since he had challenged her with a kiss. When she had left abruptly, he had decided it was prudent to let her go. However, an hour later, he could still feel the sweet echo of her lips against his own and visualize the smoky awareness of passion in her eyes. The look had been grudging, and had told him she was not pleased that he had fanned the flames of her desires. The hour grew late, and few guests remained at the reception. Kardahl and Jessica had departed some time ago for their honeymoon, and to privately celebrate the news that they would have a child. He envied his brother and the happiness he had found. And, while Malik did not expect lightning to strike twice, as the saying went, it was his wish to know contentment with Beth. Already he liked her, and if the kiss they had shared was any indication there would be satisfaction in the physical aspect of their union.

Just then he saw her across the room, touching a flute of champagne to the glass of the man who stood beside her. Looking closer, Malik recognized a friend of Kardahl's from his infamous bachelor days. Carlo Genovese, a pauper with a title he parlayed into female conquests all over the world. The rogue left a string of broken hearts wherever he went.

Although there was nothing inappropriate transpiring between them, Malik did not like Beth so near another man—a womanizer who would use her without a second thought. Despite her admission that she had once been in love, he did not believe that she was worldly enough to withstand a determined assault from such a notorious scoundrel. Malik acknowledged a vague awareness that his reaction was more than an overly developed sense of protection. He recognized the unexpected and unwelcome sting of jealousy.

He crossed the room, eating up the distance to his betrothed with a longer than usual stride. He insinuated himself between Beth and the tall, muscular man with burnished brown hair and blue eyes. Sliding his arm around her waist, Malik drew her protectively to his side and felt a shiver go through her when he kissed her cheek.

He smiled tenderly at her, then met the other man's amused gaze. "Carlo, I see you have met my bride-to-be."

"Indeed, I have. You are a lucky man."

The look Carlo settled on Beth was rife with an admiration that filled Malik with the almost overwhelming urge to remove the satisfied smile from the other man's pretty face. This primitive feeling was both foreign and foolish—a thought that told him at least a part of his brain still functioned. The problem was, it was only a small part. With the majority of his mental faculties engaged in visions of violence, there was not enough left over for rational thought. This was unacceptable for a man who would lead his country.

He was held to a higher standard. The average man had the luxury of acting on his jealousy, but Malik did not. This strong reaction was a sure sign that his feelings for Beth were much more than he wished them to be.

"A lucky man," he repeated, meeting her gaze and noting the flicker of surprise at his edgy tone.

"Carlo was just telling me that he is engaged as well. To a Hungarian countess," Beth said.

With a large fortune, no doubt, Malik thought disapprovingly. But that explained the clinking of champagne glasses. "Congratulations. I wish you every happiness."

"And I you."

Malik made a show of looking around the room. "Please introduce us to her."

"To my regret, she was unable to accompany me." Carlo feigned disappointment for Beth's benefit.

"That's too bad," she said. "Have you set a date for the wedding?"

"Not yet. And you?" he asked. "Will I be returning to Bha'Khar soon, for another joyous celebration?"

Not if he could help it, Malik thought. "We have not yet selected a day. But if I have my way it will be soon."

Beth's smile faltered, and she finished the champagne in her glass without responding.

"I can understand why you would be anxious to make her yours. She is a lovely and desirable woman." Carlo bowed slightly. "Now, if you will excuse me—"

"Of course." Do not let the door hit you in the backside on your way out, Malik thought.

"Beth." Carlo kissed her hand. "It was a great pleasure to meet you."

"For me, as well."

Malik struggled with the dark emotions simmering through him before seizing a bottle of champagne and two glasses from a passing waiter. He motioned Beth to a small table in a shadowed, secluded corner of the room. After settling her in a chair, he sat across from her, the knees of his black tuxedo trousers barely brushing the satin skirt of her royal blue gown. The hour grew late, and the day had been long, but she still carried herself like a princess.

"Have I told you how beautiful you look tonight?" he asked, letting his gaze caress her cheeks, nose, chin and long, graceful neck.

"Thank you." Her smile was both pleased and shy. "But it's all about the dress and jewelry."

If only that were true. She'd look just as lovely in jeans or pants. Or nothing, he thought, his gaze lowering to the graceful curve of her breasts. The sudden vivid flash of desire stole the air from his lungs and heated his blood until it was like a fireball roaring through him.

He handed her a full glass of champagne and took one for himself, hoping it would quell this unwelcome fascination. "Let us drink to new beginnings."

His choice of words reminded him of their first kiss, of a new phase of getting to know each other—a pleasing phase, to his way of thinking.

"To beginnings." She tapped her glass to his, then took a sip.

Malik could not force his gaze from the lingering moisture on her lips. The intense desire welling inside him to kiss it away was one facet of the extreme emotion that was fast becoming a problem. It was imperative that he find something to say to her that would distract him from his deepening awareness.

"So," he said. "Is this a better time to talk about your meeting with your mother? I understand why you were unwilling to speak of it before, but it is my hope that you will feel comfortable confiding in me."

She looked around the almost empty room, as if searching for an escape route, then sighed. "It was enlightening."

"In what way?"

Her eyes lost their sparkle and turned darker, brooding, angry. "All these years I blamed my mother for leaving us—"

"Us?"

She looked momentarily startled, then said, "My sister and I."

"I keep forgetting that you have a sister."

"Yes," she said, her gaze skittering away. "It turns

out that my mother was also a victim of a man who lives by his own rules."

"The ambassador?" When she nodded, he asked, "How so?"

"He had an affair. Technically it wasn't an affair until after he married my mother. But he continued to see the woman after he'd spoken his vows. When my mother found out, she stood up to him and said she was leaving. But my father left first—with my sister and I. He kept my mother from seeing us. Because he's a powerful man, he could do that. And all this time he let me believe that she had left and didn't love me."

Malik knew the ambassador was divorced, but he had not been aware of these details. He noted the bitterness in Beth's tone and sensed that there was more she was not saying. This deeply personal revelation was an important piece in the puzzle of her reluctance to marry.

"Shall I recall the ambassador and strip him of his position and power?"

Beth looked shocked. "You could do that?"

"I will be King. As you have pointed out on more than one occasion, I can do what I like without rules to restrict my decisions."

"Wow." The sparkle returned to her eyes. "So it's true what they say?"

"And what is that?"

"Rank has its privileges."

"Indeed." He took her hand in his and brushed his thumb over her knuckles before touching his lips there. "Say the word and I will make him sorry that he hurt you."

She sighed. "I appreciate the thought. If only you were powerful enough to give me back a childhood with my mother in it. But it's too late now. I'm all grown up."

Indeed she was—a fact that continually failed to escape his notice. "I cannot give you back your childhood, but your life will go on with your mother a part of it."

"Yes. Thank you for making that so easy for me." She leaned forward and kissed his cheek.

The touch produced an odd tightness in his chest—different, more perplexing and more deeply soul-stirring than the kiss they had shared earlier. It was an act of trust from a woman he knew did not trust easily.

When she pleaded fatigue and excused herself he let her go without protest, since he required distance in order to obtain some perspective. His objective to find a distraction from his emotions had been a dismal failure. If anything, her gratitude had produced even more bewildering sensations. But he was determined to exert control over his feelings and *not* let them control him.

His destiny was to take on the arduous task of ruling Bha'Khar, making his positive mark on history. He could not afford to be distracted by anything—including love.

But his destiny also included her. Together they would guide Bha'Khar in an ever-changing and increasingly insecure world. That meant forging a close personal connection. Trust would be required, and currently she did not trust him—a state reinforced by talking with her mother. When he vowed to honor Beth always, and be faithful only to her, he *would* keep his word. There must be a way he could show her that, unlike her father and the other man she had known, he, Malik, took his promises most seriously.

And he thought he knew just the thing to demonstrate his integrity.

"And you thought I would like to see the palace harem…why?" Beth asked.

"Because it is part of my family history."

The night after the wedding, Beth stood with Malik in the hall outside his parents' suite. Dinner had been just the four of them, and very informal. She liked the King and Queen, who had embraced her warmly, like one of the family. Acceptance was a concept lacking in her life since her father had destroyed her own family, and he wouldn't know personal warmth if someone set him on fire. The thought made her sad, and the strain of pretending was wearing her out. But Malik's surprise tour had managed to spark her curiosity.

"Does the harem have a dress code?"

She glanced down at her cotton summer dress, enjoying the light coolness of the material. And the pockets. She slid her hand inside and curled her fingers around the cellphone, praying that Addie's overdue call would come and wishing she was anywhere but here.

"You look lovely, as always."

And Malik looked every inch the rogue sheikh, in his black pants and white silk shirt, with the sleeves rolled to just below his elbows. She had feelings for him that were growing hotter, stronger and deeper every day. He was even more powerful than her father, who had ruined her mother's life. The woman who fell in love with the Crown Prince was to be pitied, and Beth didn't want to be that woman. Her feelings had to be stopped, but she was afraid that would become impossible if this pretense went on much longer.

Suddenly she was hot and cold and sick to her stomach at what she was doing. She was a liar and a sneak. The only thing that soothed her was the reminder that this was all for her sister. Beth remembered that first night without their mother, how they'd clung together through the confusion and fear. Addie and Beth against the world.

Just a little longer, she thought, and put herself back in the moment. The harem. Right. A tour might just take the edge off her guilty conscience. She met Malik's gaze and decided she could picture him in a harem, choosing his woman for the night. But instead of being a detached observation, this particular vision sank its fangs into her heart.

When the elevator arrived to take them to the ground floor, he settled his hand at her waist to guide her into the mahogany and glass car. The heat of his fingers unleashed a prickling of awareness that made her body flush with heat.

"A guided tour of the history of infidelity," she mused. "I agreed that we should get to know each other to give this betrothal a chance. But maybe the royal harem is too much information?"

He grinned. "Maybe you should withhold judgment until you have seen it?"

"I'm not sure. By definition, a harem is a group of women associated with one man."

"Indeed," he agreed, too easily. He slid his hands into the pockets of his pants, which both relieved and disappointed her. "But in the old days those women included servants and female relatives."

"And mistresses."

"In the old days the more common terminology was concubine."

"Oh," she said. "That sounds ever so much more elegant. I'm feeling better about this by the second."

One of his dark eyebrows rose in question. "Has it escaped your notice that you are very swift to judge?"

She folded her arms over her chest and studied his serious expression. "That's a trick question. If I say yes, I'm agreeing that you're right about me being judgmental. If I say no, same thing. You're very clever—you know that?"

"If I say yes, I am pompous and arrogant. And saying no would just be—" He shrugged. "Wrong. Of course I am clever."

She shook her head, wanting desperately to grin. How was she supposed to resist a man who was both self-aware and able to laugh about it? He was endearingly arrogant, and that wasn't easy to pull off.

When the elevator stopped, the doors opened and Beth stepped out. At the end of a short hall Malik pulled wide a door that opened into a garden. Warm, sultry air surrounded her, along with the smell of jasmine. The palace grounds were extensive and a high stucco wall surrounded them, providing privacy in this quiet, lush place. Skillfully arranged spotlights accentuated tall palm trees, sweet-smelling flowers and flourishing greenery. Small white lights twinkled in the bushes and trees.

She gasped. "Oh, my. I had no idea something so beautiful was hidden within the palace."

"I have been saving this to impress you."

"Big mistake."

He arched an eyebrow. "You are unimpressed?"

"No. Quite the contrary. Your mistake is in showing me cars and planes and boats on my first tour instead of this. It's magical."

"The perfect place for a harem."

"Thanks for reminding me," she said wryly. "I almost forgot."

"Come." He held out a hand. "I will show you."

It was more intimate than taking his arm, but she couldn't deny herself the chance to touch him. Hand in hand, they walked down a stone path through the lush vegetation. She knew little about flowers except that these vivid pink, deep red and vibrant orange blossoms were exquisite.

At the end of the path they stopped in front of a

structure with pale salmon-colored stucco walls and a red tiled roof. Beautiful stained glass filled the windows. It would be exquisite inside, with the light shining through, but at the moment everything was dark.

"You didn't pay the electric bill?" she asked.

After shooting her a patiently amused look, he removed a large key from his pocket and slid it into the appropriate opening in the door, then turned it.

"It's locked? You don't want anyone to steal your women?" She put her hand on his arm. "The women are prisoners?"

Without responding, he settled his hand on the ornate brass handle and pushed the door wide. Reaching inside, he flipped a switch, and an overhead chandelier blazed with light, illuminating a circular foyer with a floor made of stones that formed a picture of palms, peacocks and a princess with a crown. The walls were painted a delicate shade of peach that was hardly more than a blush.

Beth was speechless as she followed Malik from room to room, taking in the beautiful stone floor, the marble baths with gold fixtures, and the furniture covered with sheets. The last room was a bedroom as big as her whole apartment in Los Angeles. It held a four-poster bed with a matching armoire, and a gold brocade-covered chaise. This had to be harem heaven.

"So, is this where the King comes to—relax?" Even if she'd wanted it to, her sarcasm wouldn't behave.

Malik's expression was gravely sincere as he

shook his head. "The harem has been locked up and abandoned since the time of my great-grandfather."

"Really?"

He glanced around and nodded. "It seems that after marrying his betrothed the two actually fell in love. As the story was told to me by my father, my great-grandmother stood up to the King and told him in no uncertain terms that she was in love with him and there would be no other woman but her in his bed. If he was not in agreement about this, she would accept it in time, but she would disappear from his life. She would not stand meekly by, knowing she did not possess his whole heart."

"Wow."

"Indeed."

"She sounds like a strong and determined lady."

"I would not disagree."

"So what did your great-grandfather say to that?" she asked, her curiosity acutely aroused by the guts and bravado of this woman.

Malik's mouth curved up slightly. "He assured her that he wanted no one else."

"Talk is cheap," she pointed out.

"And actions speak louder than words," he countered, seeing her cliché and raising her with one of his own. "Great-grandfather disbanded the harem and locked it up. It has been abandoned for these many years."

"Hmm."

"But there is a rumor that they often sneaked away to this room when they wished to…"

"Play the King and the concubine?" she said with a grin.

"Indeed." A gleam stole into his eyes that made her heart beat faster. Then he rubbed his thumb over the carving in one of the bedposts and his smile disappeared. "The two were happily married for more than fifty years, passing on within weeks of each other. As if living without the love of their life was intolerable."

She sighed. "It's a beautiful story."

"Not just a story—my history," he corrected. "And ever since that time, along with the revered tradition of contracting a marriage, the men in my family have practiced fidelity and held it sacred."

Her gaze skipped over his face, noting the solemn gravity in his expression. For someone he deemed quick to judgment, she was at a loss to judge whether or not he was telling her the truth. A little while ago she'd thought, for the gazillionth time, how much she hated this pretense—but not as much as she resented the man who had stolen her trusting nature, or the one who'd stolen her childhood. Her instincts were telling her that Malik was sincere, but she'd chosen so poorly in the past that she couldn't put any faith in her instincts.

But it wasn't instinct telling her that she wished she'd met Malik under different circumstances. It was her heart.

Malik studied her expectantly before saying, "You are uncharacteristically silent."

"I'm just trying to reconcile the intriguing idea of

a woman controlling a man. A powerful man. It's astonishing to me."

"A man, even a king, is still just a man."

"And you expect me to believe that the King of Bha'Khar voluntarily turned his back on all this—" She swung her arm out in a sweeping gesture that encompassed the large, elegant and ultimately sexy room. More than a room. A love-nest. "Because the woman who was chosen for him demanded it?"

"He was not simply the King of Bha'Khar. He was a man in love."

"Still—"

"Do not underestimate the power a woman holds over a man." His sudden frown and harsh tone said the observation was anything but romantic.

By his own admission he had been a man in love, and he didn't want to repeat the experience. Beth knew her own reasons, but he hadn't revealed his.

"What did you do for the woman you loved?" she asked.

"I do not wish to speak of it."

He walked out of the room and her curiosity started humming. She wasn't letting him off the hook this time. Following quickly, she caught up with him as he walked out through the harem's front door. On the stone path in the magical garden she said, "Malik, don't shut me out."

He hesitated, then stopped. Tension stiffened his shoulders before he turned to her. "I simply wish to forget."

"We're getting to know each other. I told you

about me. Now I need to know what happened to you."

He shook his head. "I do not—"

"You ask for my trust. It's impossible to give that to you unless you share. Not just your family's story. Your own personal experience."

He looked down for several moments, his expression darkly intense, before he met her gaze and sighed. "All right. I will tell you about the pretender who betrayed me."

CHAPTER EIGHT

"I FELL in love with a woman who was pretending to be something she was not."

That hot, cold, nauseous feeling from earlier swept over Beth again and made her lightheaded. Was he talking about her? Was he on to her pretense? Did he love her?

When the roaring in her ears faded, she was able to think more clearly. A guilty conscience certainly made one self-centered. But this couldn't be about her, because there was only bitterness in his tone. If he knew what she was doing he'd be furious. This was about the woman who had turned him off to love.

"Where did you meet her?"

"Right here in the palace."

"Here?" she whispered, glancing around at the perfect garden, with its twinkling lights, trees and brightly colored flowers. It was a place of tranquility; deception would defile the magic. *She* defiled it.

"Not here," he amended, following her gaze. "She

worked in the business wing of the palace. An assistant to an assistant."

"Isn't the staff subject to background checks?"

"Yes. But she was just out of college. There was no professional employment record yet. No one knew of her real job."

"Which was?"

"Tabloid reporter." His expression was grim.

"What happened?" The question was automatic, but Beth knew what was coming.

"She first captured my notice while picking up a stack of files in the hallway outside my office." The expression in his eyes would freeze water in July. "It never occurred to me that she had no business there. I simply stopped to assist her."

Because he's a nice man, she thought. Polite. Thoughtful. Kind. She was incredibly sorry she'd opened this can of worms, but there was no turning back now. "Then what?"

"There were more 'accidental' meetings. I began to notice how lovely she was, and before long I began to seek her out."

Even though you were engaged? she wanted to ask. But it was best not to go there, since she'd confessed to a love affair of her own. "And she didn't discourage it?"

"No." His look was wry. "We talked, and I found her to be a good listener. An admirable trait, I believed, not realizing it is a reporter's way, and she was exploiting the situation. She asked questions that I perceived as easing the burden I carried. In truth she was taking notes for a story entitled *The King-to-Be and I: Sex and the Sheikh.*"

"There was a public scandal," Beth guessed.

"Actually, no. Because she had signed a confidentiality agreement, I used my extensive power and influence to suppress the story. The private reality was worse. The King was furious."

If anyone understood how much it hurt when you disappointed your father it was her. "But how could you have known?"

"I should have. I am held to a higher standard— a fact that I was reminded of. The imposter insinuated herself into my life to further her journalistic career."

"It's appalling that someone would use you that way."

"*That* way? Is there a good way to use someone?" His voice was soft and deceptively calm, deep and dangerous.

The sick feeling was back. "I just meant that in rare instances there's justification for certain actions."

"Never," he said. "Doing the wrong thing for the right reason is still wrong. Any argument to the contrary is simply splitting hairs. Lying is never defensible. Of all people you should know, courtesy of the cad who turned you against love."

He had her there.

But the look on his face scared her.

"What, Malik?" The muscle jerking in his jaw told her there was something even worse than falling in love with a schemer. "What else happened?"

She put her fingers on his arm, the warmth of his skin reminding her of his vulnerability, making her want to put her arms around the flesh-and-blood man who'd been used and hurt. She understood how that felt, and she wanted to comfort him.

"There is nothing."

She tilted her head to the side as she studied him. "For a man who has just preached the virtues of telling the truth, you're dangerously close to a do-as-I-say-not-as-I-do attitude. What aren't you telling me?"

He blew out a long breath before taking her hand and nestling it between his own. "I cared deeply for this woman and found the notion of marrying anyone else intolerable. When I approached the King in defiance, he had her investigated and the true nature of her interest was uncovered."

"You were prepared to abandon years of tradition for her?"

"Yes." His mouth pulled tight while his eyes smoldered.

"You must have loved her a great deal."

"And the memory makes me feel foolish and furious in equal measure."

"But it's not your fault," she protested.

"As I was the fool who fell for her ruse, who else is there to blame? It was a hard lesson in the treachery of women, and it highlighted the value of a tradition that allows those wiser than myself to choose an appropriate wife for the future King."

No wonder he was in favor of this betrothal. It was his duty to marry, and this was an expedient way to find a safe wife. The sick feeling inside her grew into a dark and ugly knot. If anyone understood his hesitation, it was her. She'd been deceived and used. Now she was doing it to him, and she just couldn't stand it anymore.

It was time to come clean.

This charade had gone far enough, and words of confession were on the tip of her tongue. The best way to stop her growing feelings would be to tell him the truth, then he would hate and shun her. But something deep inside her cried out against that and made her hesitate. Before she could get the words out, a cellphone rang.

Beth reached into her pocket and pulled hers out. No call. When she looked up, Malik had his open. He answered, listened then hung up.

He met her gaze and there was regret in his eyes. "There is something that requires my attention."

"Now?"

He nodded. "I apologize."

"The Crown Prince's work is never done?" she said.

"Indeed." He settled his hand at her waist. "I will see you upstairs."

"If it's all the same to you, I'd like to stay here in the garden. It's peaceful and quiet, and I could use a lot of both."

"You are certain?"

She nodded. "I can find my way back."

"Very well." He looked around. "I, too, find this place soothing."

"It's perfect."

He nodded, then was gone. She was relieved. As much as she needed to be straight with him, this was the wrong place to say the words. To mar the flawlessness of this haven would only add to her list of sins. It was long enough already.

She wandered along the stone path, past the harem. She walked for what seemed like hours, searching for calm, tranquility, composure. Soothing of the soul.

It never happened, and she finally realized she wouldn't find absolution until she owned up to her lie. She headed for the elevator that would take her to her suite, then she heard the ring of her cell.

She pulled it out of her pocket and answered. "Hello?"

"Beth? It's Addie. I'm in Bha'Khar."

Beth rode in the back of the car Malik had put at her disposal. They had met for lunch, and when she'd mentioned seeing her mother he'd offered transportation and a driver. This time it was only half a lie, since she *was* meeting Addie at their mother's house. But she was splitting hairs and desperately tired of it. Now that Addie was here Beth could finally stop deceiving Malik.

Suddenly it hit her that she wouldn't see him anymore. Her heart seemed to stop beating for a split second, then started again, generating a rushing sound in her ears. All she would have were memories. Of his kisses, of the intimate tour of the harem, the perfect garden where he'd told her his darkest secret.

Her mother's words came to mind.

Are you becoming too fond of this man? Will you be able to let him go without regret? Without hurting your heart?

Now Beth knew the answers to those questions. Yes. No. And emphatically no.

The car pulled to a stop in front of the square white stucco house with the flat roof. This time, instead of resentment and dread at the prospect of seeing her mother, she felt eagerness and warmth. And love, she realized.

The driver opened the door and she slid out. "There's no need to wait. I'll be here for a while."

He bowed slightly. "As you wish."

When he had driven away, she went to the door and knocked. Addie answered and greeted her with a grin. "Hi, Beth."

Beth looked at her mirror image. Same shiny shoulder-length dark hair. Same brown eyes with gold flecks. Same brows, cheeks, mouth and chin. She'd missed her sister terribly and opened her arms for a hug. "It's so good to see you."

Sameera stood behind them and smiled, even as she discreetly brushed her cheeks and tried not to reveal her tears. Her voice was steady when she said, "*Good* does not even begin to describe how it feels to see both of my girls together after so many years."

"Mama knew me right away."

Beth sniffed. "Me, too. I've got that birthmark and you don't."

"She told me." Addie pulled her mother into their hug. "I know what happened with her and Father, too."

"Let us not speak of that time," Sameera said. "We will sit and talk about now."

"Good idea," Beth agreed.

When they were settled in the living room, with a tray of sandwiches and lemonade and their mother between them on the couch, Beth figured now was as good a time as any to talk about the situation with Malik.

"Addie, what happened with the guy? Since you're here, I guess you've had enough time?"

"Oh, yeah." The tone, the sigh, the flash of pain in eyes identical to her own were not a good sign. "Turns out he's married. I was so stupid."

"Jerk," Beth said.

Sameera said something in Bha'Kharian that burned her ears and made Beth blink, just before she grinned at her sister. "I couldn't have said it better myself. Go, Mom."

"It is not something I would say in mixed company. But we are three women here," she said, putting a hand on each of them.

Beth squeezed her fingers. "We are. Finally." She looked across her mother and watched Addie finish a sandwich. Apparently the jerk had stolen her trust but left her appetite intact. "So, I'll back you up when you tell Father you're not going through with the betrothal?"

"That's not necessary."

"Are you sure you want to face him by yourself?"

Beth asked. She would face a dragon for this beloved sister. In fact, she was used to it.

"I don't have to."

"Mom?" she said, glancing at Sameera.

"Do not look at me."

"Addie? What are you saying?"

"I'm going to marry the Crown Prince, as arranged," Addie said. "There's no reason to say anything to Father."

For the second time that day Beth's heart stopped, then started pounding. "Even now you've found out that I was right? That powerful men don't think basic morality applies to them?"

"What difference does it make?" Addie shrugged.

"It's wrong on so many levels." She looked at their mother. "Tell her it's wrong."

Sameera shook her head even as she looked worried. "I cannot interfere. Addie is a grown woman and must make up her own mind."

"Addie, you shouldn't have to do this. It's wrong," Beth said again, hating the helplessness she was feeling.

"Not if I go into it with my eyes open. Not if my expectations are proportionate to the circumstances."

"And what are your expectations?"

"Marriage. Children."

It was what Malik wanted, too, Beth knew. She also knew, after spending time with him and his family, that an arranged marriage could be a happy one. "Is that all?"

Addie wiped her mouth with a napkin. "At

boarding school I was educated in etiquette and the social graces. There were classes in protocol for all occasions. I was trained to be the Queen of Bha'Khar and serve my people at the side of the King. I expect to do a good job of it."

"What about personal happiness?" Beth demanded.

Even as she could see her own going down the tubes, she was concerned that her sister would be trapped in a situation that would eventually make her miserable.

"Many women find personal happiness and satisfaction in a job well done. I expect that I will do the same. If I'm very lucky, His Royal Highness and I will grow fond of each other."

That sound only Beth could hear was probably her heart cracking. And it begged the question: why was she trying to talk her sister out of this marriage? Was it for Addie's sake? Or her own? So now she was a selfish, self-centered liar.

"Addie, think about this—"

"You believe I haven't?" She blew out a long breath. "It's a long plane ride, Bethie. I thought about little else. And the thing is, I just found my mother, after many painful years without her. I know what it's like not to have a parent, and now I have them both. I'm not going to destroy my relationship with Father. I have no illusions. I know he's not perfect. But I love him and I need him in my life."

Beth knew her twin's stubbornness better than anyone, and she recognized when to stop fighting.

Beth's appetite had disappeared. She set the plate with her uneaten sandwich on the coffee table, then studied her sister. "Okay, then. We need to coordinate the switch for you to take your rightful place. Our hair is the same. All we need to do is exchange clothes and no one will know the difference. I'll brief you on the palace layout and what's happened since I've been here."

Leaving out the kiss, of course. There were some things her twin was simply better off not knowing. Beth couldn't think about Malik kissing Addie. It was too complicated, and it hurt more than she'd believed possible.

"What's he like?" Addie asked, her voice laced with curiosity along with a hint of apprehension.

"Who?"

"The Crown Prince."

"Malik," she corrected. "It's his given name, and what he prefers to be called in private."

"Malik," Addie said, testing it out. "What else can you tell me?"

That he doesn't want to love any woman. That he believes in the tradition of arranged marriage and relies on those wiser than himself to choose someone he could trust. That royal men are faithful and constant. He's supportive and has a jealous streak that had thrilled her. He makes a woman's heart beat faster and kisses like a dream. He makes her want the way she's never wanted before. Following tradition could break a girl's heart.

"Bethie?"

She looked up and met the knowing gaze of her mother. "Sorry. I was zoning out."

"Your sister asked you what her intended is like," Sameera said.

"Where to start?" Beth shrugged. "He's handsome."

"I've seen pictures," Addie assured her.

"They don't do him justice. He's much better looking in person."

"Okay. What else do I need to know?"

"He's nice, actually. Much nicer than I thought he would be." Much, much nicer.

"That's good to know. Do you like him?" Addie asked.

Like him? It was so much more than like, Beth realized. So much more that she wasn't willing to define what she felt with a word. But *like* didn't do justice to what she felt any more than photos captured the integrity of the man.

"More important, *you'll* like him," Beth finally said.

He was perfect for Addie and she for him. They would be the perfect couple in their perfect palace with their perfect children. Addie would be perfectly happy and Beth would be perfectly miserable.

"Now, then," she said, burying her resentment as deeply as possible. "I'll make some notes for you—and a diagram of the palace as best I can. And other things you need to know."

"Good. But I'll probably need some time to study your notes." Addie looked at their mother.

Beth glanced between the two women. "How much time? You could be in the palace by dinnertime, right?"

"The thing is, Bethie, I just met Mama again after a long separation."

"So come and visit every day," Beth suggested.

"Okay. That's a good idea." Addie caught her top lip between her teeth. "But once I switch places with you there will be so many distractions. A role to play. A wedding to plan. People to meet."

"This is what you've been trained for," Beth reminded her. "Your place is on the world stage."

"Yes. And I'm looking forward to it." Her voice only caught a little. No one else would have noticed. "But first I'd like to spend a little time getting to know Mama again."

Beth stared at her. She wanted more time? Did she have any idea what she was asking? Of course not. How could she? Because Beth hadn't told her about kissing Malik, or how it had filled her with an ache for more. She hadn't shared her growing need to be with him, to tell him small unimportant stories over breakfast and make dates for lunch and dinner. She could never reveal that one look into the eyes of the man Addie was going to marry had trapped Beth in a current of desire so strong she couldn't find her way out and didn't really care to. It had taken everything she had just to show up here. How could she tell Addie any of that, or how hard this was?

The truth was, in addition to Malik, Beth was now lying to her sister.

Switching places had seemed so easy, so harmless, but now it came under the heading of "didn't think it through." She couldn't have known that Malik would capture her emotions so fast, so intensely. She had to end it now—today—if she was to have any hope of salvaging her heart.

"I think it would be best to make the switch now," Beth said. "I'd like to spend some time with Mom again, too."

"But you'll have plenty of time," Addie pointed out. "I'm only asking for a few days. A week at most. Please, Beth. I may never get an opportunity like this, and I've lost so much time with her already."

Oh, how Beth hated the fact that she couldn't resist Addie's pleading look, or say no when her twin asked in just that needy tone of voice. The patterns of childhood and standing up for her vulnerable sister were horribly difficult to break, even though this felt so completely wrong. But the truth was worse. She was desperately glad to have more time with Malik. She was grateful for the reprieve and dreaded it at the same time.

Beth sighed. "All right, Addie. A week. Tops."

CHAPTER NINE

THE Gulfstream taxied down Bha'Khar's runway and picked up speed before taking off and gaining altitude. Malik's gaze never left Beth's pale face. She sat in the tufted leather seat beside him, staring out the window.

"You are not a nervous flyer?" he asked.

Her gaze shifted to his and her expression was wry. "If I were, asking me now would be like closing the barn door after the cow got out."

He thought about the colloquialism and decided it was very visual and most descriptive. "I will take that to mean that flying does not make you nervous."

"You take it right." She looked out the window again.

Her spirited comment had given him hope that her pensiveness of the last several days had disappeared, but hope died when he noted the tension gathered in her slender neck and shoulders. It bothered him to see her this way, and it disturbed him even more that he'd noticed and was bothered at all. Especially that he'd been bothered enough to rearrange his schedule for this trip, to lift her spirits. It annoyed him that he missed her energetic, provocative personality.

"You have not asked where we are going," he pointed out.

"You like surprises. I figured I'd let you play this one out."

"Are you not the least bit curious?"

"Of course I am. Who wouldn't be? I'd have to be on life support and in a coma not to wonder."

"Would you like a hint?"

"Would you like to give me one?" she asked.

"Do you always answer a question with a question?"

"Do you?" she retorted.

He grinned. Maybe he was getting somewhere. "We are going to a city in Europe."

"That narrows it down." She angled her body toward him, which was a start.

"The country in which this city is located is famous for its food and wine, museums and scenery."

"Not narrowing it down, Your Highness," she chided.

"It is called the city of lights."

"Paris?" Her dark eyebrows rose in surprise.

"Indeed."

"Oh, Malik—" For a moment her eyes shone as brightly as stars in an ink-black sky, and a pleased smile curved the corners of her mouth. Then her delight receded. "I wish you hadn't done this."

"Why?"

"I could ask you the same thing. Why? Why did you do this for me?"

"Is it so difficult to believe that I wish to make a grand gesture to surprise you?"

Just then the captain turned off the "Fasten Seatbelts" sign and Malik released his, as did Beth. He stood and extended his hand. "Come, I will show you around."

She put her fingers in his and let him pull her to her feet. The plane bounced once and sent her bumping into him. When his arms came around her to steady her a flicker of awareness came into her eyes, before she stepped deliberately away.

"This isn't the plane I flew on when I came to Bha'Khar. How many do you have?"

"Several. For their honeymoon, Kardahl and Jessica are using the one you have seen. It is bigger, but I believe this one is more intimate."

She looked away, letting her gaze roam over the two groupings of brown leather seats. In the plane's main body there was a conference table, with swivel armchairs surrounding it.

"This is nice."

"Let me show you the rest."

He escorted her to the rear, where a small area was set off with a twin bed that pulled out into a king-size bed. In the bathroom there was a marble-enclosed shower stall, and a sink with gold fixtures. Berber carpet cushioned the floor beneath their feet.

She looked around, clearly impressed. "It's pretty amazing what can be done with a small space."

"No expense was spared," he agreed.

They stood facing each other in the narrow

doorway to the bedroom. Soft terrycloth robes hung on hooks beside them.

"Why did you do this?" she asked.

"Because I could. And I admit I like luxury."

"No," she said. "I didn't mean plan the amenities on the plane. I meant it's very sweet of you to surprise me with a trip to Paris. I can't help wondering why."

"It is to prove to you that I am indeed 'a catch.'"

She closed her eyes for a moment, looking miserable. And Malik was at a loss to understand her reaction. He had deliberately baited her, his calculated remark intended to instigate a spirited discussion—something he had sorely missed the last several days.

"What is it, Beth? What troubles you?"

"Nothing. I'm fine. I don't mean to behave like an ungrateful witch. This was a really nice surprise. Thank you." She smiled, but it was nothing more than a curving of lips and did not reach her eyes.

"Something is wrong. I can feel it. Did all go well when you saw your mother?"

Her gaze snapped to his, and a look that could only be described as guilty jumped into her eyes. "Of course. Everything is fine."

"Then why do you look as if you have lost your dearest friend?"

Her expression told him he had surprised her with his insight. "You're imagining things. I don't look like that."

"You are wrong."

"You don't know me as well as you think you do," she said.

"I know you better than you realize." He took a step closer, trapping her between the wall and his body. "I know your moods, and your expressions. I sense when you are happy or hiding something."

"Oh?" Her voice was hardly more than a whisper.

He nodded. "And right now you are trying to convince me that there is nothing troubling you when I know something is on your mind. And I think I know what it is."

"Y-you do?" Her dark eyes grew wide.

"It is the wedding. Am I not correct?"

"In a manner of speaking."

Her confirmation did not remove the dubious expression in her eyes, and he wanted very much to do that. "Do not worry. All will be fine."

"That's easy for you to say."

She looked so distressed and dispirited. He felt it deep inside, in a place he had closed off, a place where he did not want to feel anything at all. Not again. The distraction was unwelcome, yet he could not seem to make it go away. This abject unhappiness in Beth was more than he could stand. He did the only thing he could think of to erase it from her lovely face.

Malik pressed his body gently to hers and took her face in his hands, tunneling his fingers in her silky dark hair. "Do not worry, my sweet. I will do my best to make you happy."

Malik lowered his head and settled his mouth

against hers. At the first touch he felt the lust tighten within him, like fingers curling into a shaking fist, desperate to punch through. Skimming his tongue over her cool lips, he encouraged them to warmth and willingness. When she opened to him, a soft purr of surrender escaped her throat, and his need churned outward until it scratched to the surface, sizzled and stayed.

He could not stop the need to touch her, to fill his palms with the beautiful soft mounds of her breasts through her silk blouse. Her moan of pleasure fueled his desire. Her head tilted to the side, giving his eager mouth unfettered access to the smooth, sensuous column of her throat. He brushed his lips over her soft flesh and heard her breathy groan. When he lifted his head and filled his gaze with the erotic picture of her lowered lashes, her mouth parted and breath straining, he couldn't stop himself. He lifted her into his arms.

As if against her will, her own arms came slowly, hesitantly around his neck, and her fingers slid into his hair. He had never been more grateful to have the "small" jet as when he turned and in one fluid movement set her on the bed. When he came down beside her, she gasped. With thumb and forefinger, he started to undo the top button on her blouse. He smiled with satisfaction when he brushed his mouth over her throat and felt her shiver of response.

"You are so beautiful," he breathed against her skin. There was a birthmark behind her right ear— something he had not noticed before, probably hidden from him in the moonlight. He kissed the spot and felt her shiver, sending a shaft of heat straight to his groin. The memory of her under the stars, the feel of her in his arms, the sweet scent of her filling his head all rolled into a knot of need that could not be ignored. "I can wait no longer to make you mine."

She froze in his arms and went still. "Malik—"

He lifted his head and saw the shadows return to replace the passion in her eyes. "What is it?"

"I can't— We can't—"

"I *can*. I want you."

She pulled out of his arms and sat up. "This is wrong."

"If feels completely right," he said, raking his fingers through his hair.

"But I'm not— You should know—"

"What?" When he sat up, she slid off the bed and stood as far from him as the small cabin allowed.

"I think this—" She held out a hand and indicated the bed. "Sex—should wait until after the wedding."

He let out a long breath as a string of curses in several languages raced through his mind. "What if I do not wish to wait?"

"What if I do?" Her breathing was unsteady.

So was his willpower, and he let out a long breath. "I would be a cad to ignore your wishes. But there is something I wish from you in exchange."

"Anything," she agreed quickly.

"We must set a date for the wedding. And it must be soon."

* * *

"I had to do some fast talking to get him to hold off pushing for a wedding date," Beth told her mother.

"This is why after returning from Paris you are insisting that your sister switch places right away?"

"Yes."

That, and so much more. A day and night in Paris after that kiss on the plane had been torture. That was why Beth had insisted her twin make the switch. They needed to do it before Beth couldn't do it at all. Malik cared enough to cheer her up, and that was as seductive as his kiss. For a girl who had never been loved, it was a feeling she never wanted to give up. So, before she changed her mind, she'd told Addie it was time.

Now she was standing with her mother in the small bedroom that Addie had just vacated and Beth was going to take over for a few days, until she went back to the States. After a briefing, along with notes and a crudely drawn map of the palace, her twin was going to keep a dinner date with her betrothed.

Beth did her level best to keep her envy in check, but she was a dismal failure. Malik was the most romantic man she'd ever met, and Addie was in for a treat as he swept her away. The two of them would be very happy, and Beth was trying to be happy for them. Clearly it would take time and a lot of work. Therapy would no doubt be involved.

Her mother walked further into the room and sat on the bed beside the pile of Beth's clothes. "What else are you running away from, Bethie?"

"What else could there be?" She folded a T-shirt, then held it protectively against her as she met her mother's insightful gaze.

Sameera sighed. "I cannot help feeling that this situation is all my fault."

"That's just silly," Beth said. "You didn't arrange for Addie to marry the Prince."

"No. But I was against it from the beginning. If I had been stronger… If I had not let your father walk all over me from the moment we met… Had I but asserted myself, so much unhappiness could have been avoided." She looked at Beth, and the sadness in her dark eyes was palpable. "Especially for you and your sister."

"How?" Beth sat on the bed beside her.

"I should have put my foot down and forbade this marriage. I would have been in your life for advice and to support you. I could, perhaps, have helped you avoid the painful experience that makes you wary of love."

"I'm not sure it would have made a difference, Mom."

"Maybe." Sameera sighed. "Mutual respect is one of love's building blocks, and your father never respected me."

"I don't think he respects anyone but the King. And possibly Malik because he will be King."

"Powerful men," her mother agreed. "And your father desperately wishes to be in their ranks."

"I think that's why it's so important to him that Addie marries the Prince. He doesn't care about her happiness at all."

"And I fear that Addie does not possess the personality and disposition that will make a success of the arrangement. If I learned anything from my unhappiness with your father, it is that a powerful man needs a woman who is his equal."

Beth thought about that, among other things. She'd gone toe to toe with Malik and he didn't seem to mind. In fact, he gave every indication that he thoroughly enjoyed their verbal sparring. And that was not all.

The hot kisses they'd shared on the plane and under the Bha'Kharian moon had been more than enjoyable. They'd been full of lust and promise. And that was what made her sad. Beth felt such a connection with Malik. She'd come to know him pretty well. Power was part of his heritage, but he was also good and kind. Everything she'd told her sister. And more.

Sameera put a hand on her arm. "What are you thinking, Bethie?"

"Addie is quiet and shy, and a good person. You're right about mutual respect being the cornerstone of a successful relationship, and Malik *is* a man worthy of respect. He'll take good care of her." She recalled what he'd said about being faithful to his wife and something painful tightened inside her. "Addie is a lucky woman. I think they'll be very happy together."

Her mother studied her. "Another question that plagues me is whether or not you can be happy for them."

Beth remembered watching the car drive away with her sister inside, taking her to Malik. It was all part of the plan. A deep, hopeless ache opened up a dark, empty place inside her that she somehow knew could never be filled. Unfortunately the plan had never included Beth developing serious feelings for the man her sister was going to marry.

"Of course I can be happy for them," she said, with as much sincerity as she could rally. "Why would you ask?"

"Because I think you have fallen in love with him yourself."

"Really, Mom. His Highness the hunk? He's engaged to my sister. That would be wrong—"

Beth flashed back to the royal garden and Malik's words when he confided his dark secret. He'd told her there was never a good reason for lying. The wrong thing for the right reason was still wrong. What her father had done to Sameera was wrong, and it had cost Beth her mother's wisdom and counsel. Now they had another chance at a relationship and it would be worse than wrong not to tell her the truth.

Beth looked up and met her mother's sympathetic gaze. "There's a possibility—maybe remote, maybe not—that I have developed some…emotions for Malik."

Beth refused to call it love. If she didn't think it, maybe it wasn't so.

"I think you should tell him the truth."

"Out of the question."

"Why?"

"Why? Because Addie's going to marry him. On the rebound, but it's her choice. She's perfect for him. She's obedient. I'm willful. She's demure. I can be a little mouthy. She can plan a reception fit for royalty and I can barely put together a pizza party for friends. Malik will be a good husband to her, and I won't do anything to interfere with her happiness."

No matter how much she might want to. Not because she believed Malik was one of those men who lived by his own rules and would be unfaithful. Just the opposite. Against the odds, Malik had turned out to be a good man. Definitely a catch.

"What about *your* happiness?" her mother asked.

"When we meet, I'll be the sister-in-law he will become fond of."

If he found out she'd been deceiving him she would lose even that. Her heart ached and she felt sick to her stomach. This was her punishment for her sins. It was fitting, although that didn't make her feel any better. Destiny was playing out just as it was meant to: Addie and Malik together. Beth's interference changed nothing, except that she now had a battered soul to match her banged-up heart. If she'd kept her nose out of this whole thing everyone would have been better off. Not everyone, she realized. Only her. At least now Addie was choosing her destiny.

"What if he has feelings for you?" her mother asked.

Beth shook her head. "He thinks I'm Addie."

"What if he can tell the difference?"

"We've switched places before and no one ever caught on."

"There is always a first time."

"I don't think so. No one, including our father, has ever been able to tell us apart."

Sameera squeezed her hand. "No one?"

"No one—except you."

"Just so." She looked worried.

"But you're my mother. It's different."

"Is it? I had not seen you and your sister since you were small girls. And yet I knew you in a heartbeat. Even before I saw the birthmark."

"It's a mom thing."

"It's a love thing," her mother corrected. "Love sees beyond superficial features. Love looks deep and discerns the way of things. It has nothing to do with identical features and everything to do with one heart knowing another, knowing the other half of itself."

"I hope you're wrong."

Her mother didn't have such a great track record where love was concerned. And neither did Beth. Which was why she'd undertaken this charade in the first place—to keep her sister from being hurt. Boy, had that backfired. Beth had never anticipated that *she* would be the one in trouble.

But it was too late to undo what they'd done. At least one of them should get what she wanted. And, since Malik was determined not to fall in love, their ruse was safe. There would be no "love thing" to expose their pretense.

Addie was going to make an awesome queen, Beth thought. Just before the tears swimming in her eyes spilled down her cheeks.

CHAPTER TEN

WHERE was Beth?

Like a caged tiger, Malik impatiently prowled the stone path in front of the harem, a single red rose in his hand. It was not like her to be late. He had called to change the place where she would join him and she had agreed. But unease had settled over him after talking to her. There had been something different in her voice, a tone that he did not recognize. No tart comment about meeting at the harem—something he had anticipated with eagerness. Her docile compliance was out of character. Whatever had been troubling her was still unresolved.

Indeed, he remembered the panic that had jumped into her eyes when on the way to Paris he had suggested setting a date for their wedding. Spending time with her in the city of lights had not dulled his desire. Quite the contrary. He was anxious to make her his in every way. But her agitation had been unmistakable, and he was afraid she was planning to withdraw from the betrothal.

Malik tightened his grip on the rose, and one of the thorns pricked him as surely as the notion of Beth leaving. He did not like either sensation, but was most troubled by the latter. He very much wished to marry her. Once the ceremony had taken place and the honeymoon had been accomplished, his unwanted emotions for her would cease to be a distraction. The serenity of his life would prevail once again.

He heard the sound of heels clicking on the stone path and was irritated at the great relief pouring through him. Yet he could not suppress it either. His feelings for Beth had grown strong, despite his efforts to keep them in check. He resolved to work harder. The King had pounded home the lesson that no problem was insurmountable with hard work.

He stood in front of the unlocked harem door and waited for her to join him. "Beth—"

"Your Highness." She nodded politely and linked her fingers in front of her.

His brows drew together. She rarely addressed him in such a formal way—unless she was teasing, as she had been on the plane several days ago. Then, instead of impeccable formality, there had been a great deal of sarcasm surrounding the words. It was like a man and a woman, an ordinary couple, bantering. Advance and retreat.

Foreplay.

This woman in front of him now was icy with reserve.

"Have I done something to offend?" he asked.

She looked up with the dismayed expression of someone who had erred. "No. Of course not—Malik."

His name on her lips was uncomfortable, and that was so very different from the passion in her voice when she had whispered it as he kissed her. A thorn pricked him again, and he remembered the token of his affection.

He held it out. "I brought this for you."

"Thank you." She smiled.

"Take care with the thorns. Apparently not all were removed, as promised."

She sniffed the red blossom, just beginning to open. "It's lovely. And very thoughtful of you."

"I am a thoughtful man." He waited for a retort. Something about his lack of humility uttered in a wry and sarcastic tone.

"You are, indeed." She smiled, but an aura of formality prevented the warmth from reaching her eyes.

"I have taken the liberty of having dinner brought here," he said.

"As you wish."

He'd expected a verbal salvo, and was profoundly disappointed when he did not hear it. Puzzled, he opened the door and let her precede him inside, confused by the change in her. She never missed an opportunity to challenge him, and he had just given her an opening that she did not take.

Now she looked around, as if she had never seen this place before. "It's beautiful, Malik. How lovely the way the colors of the stained-glass window are reflected on the marble floor."

"It is the same as when you saw it last."

"I—I am still in awe of the beauty."

He studied her, unable to dispel the feeling that there was something different about her. Finally he led the way into the dining room, where a table for two was prepared with flowers and champagne. The diamond brilliance of the chandelier above was muted for romance, as instructed. He took the already opened bottle from the silver bucket and poured golden liquid into two flutes.

"To us," he said.

"A long and happy life."

"So, I take it you have no objection to having dinner here in the harem?"

"Of course not." She took a delicate sip of her drink.

No pithy comment about his women locked away. No wry question about them "relaxing." No tongue-in-cheek remark about playing the Crown Prince and the concubine.

Malik continued to scrutinize her in the subdued light. He had seen her in the sunlight, by moon's light and in every type of illumination in between. He knew her face with his eyes and fingers and mouth. Somehow this was Beth's face, but subtly altered. Her cheeks were more angular, less soft. Her chin was not quite so stubborn. Her eyes were the same dark brown, but there was no warmth, no mischief to add fire to the golden specks, no animation in them.

Was it cosmetics? He had seen the changes a woman could effect with the judicious application of eyeshadow and blush.

"You are uncharacteristically quiet," he said.

"I do apologize. Is there something you wish to discuss?"

The last time he had made that observation within these walls a lively discussion had ensued, producing his confession of past foolishness. As he continued to study her the hair at his nape prickled and a bad feeling spread through him.

There was something he must know.

He took her glass and set it on the table beside his own. Then he framed her face in his hands and lowered his mouth to hers. There was no softening of lips, no sigh of surrender, no heat and burning desire. He brushed her hair behind her ear, intending to kiss the birthmark he had so recently discovered. It was not there.

He lifted his head and glared at her. "Who are you?"

"I don't know what you mean. Malik, I—"

"You are not Beth. You look like her, but—" The angry haze cleared just enough. "You are her sister."

She recoiled as if he had raised his hand to strike her, then had the look of a felon caught in a crime. "Yes, her twin."

Not so identical, he thought, as an icy cold crept through him. "What treachery is this? She was so against our betrothal that she has pressed you into service to take her place?"

"No, Your Highness. It wasn't like that at all."

"Then tell me how it was."

She twisted her fingers together and her lips trembled. "I am Adina Farrah."

Shock numbed him. "You are my betrothed?"

"Yes."

"And Beth?"

"My sister Alina. From early childhood she was called Beth because our names sounded too much alike."

"At least she told the truth about something," he muttered.

"Do not blame Beth," she urged. "This is all my fault."

"Oh?" How could he sound so calm when shock and betrayal filled him with such anger?

"When you decided it was time to set the marriage contract in motion, I begged Beth to take my place. So I could work through some personal issues."

"What 'personal issues' would those be?" he said, his tone cool.

"I'd met someone."

"I see."

"Don't sound like that. You don't understand. I'd never been in love, and I wanted a chance to see what it felt like."

"Then you were unsuccessful. Because there is no such thing," he said, using the heat of his anger to burn back the pain licking at the edges of his consciousness.

"You're right. The guy turned out to be a jerk."

"So now you wish to proceed with marriage to me? How noble."

She stood ramrod-straight and met his gaze. "I am ready to do my duty. My father is quite anxious for our wedding to take place. As, I understand, you are also."

Beth had passed on that information. Now he understood her panic. She was an imposter.

The first time he had been duped he had accepted responsibility and vowed he would not care again. He had been so sure that a bride chosen by his father would hold no threat that he had overlooked his contracted bride as a potential source of deception. He had been aware that she was a twin, but after meeting Beth, her charm, wit and beauty had made the information unimportant. What a fool he was!

Pain licked through him, and the flames of his anger burned higher and hotter because he could not keep it at bay.

Yet again he had been deceived by a woman he cared about deeply. This was so much worse, and he could only think that it was because he had not seen it coming. He felt more foolish, more stupid and more betrayed. This time the treachery touched more than his heart. It went all the way to his soul.

Beth walked into Malik's office after talking her way past the Communications Director, an assistant, and his personal secretary, who had all eventually waved her through because they believed she was his betrothed. After closing the door behind her, she approached the desk, knowing his eyes were watching her every step. Addie had told her everything, and now she had to explain.

"What do you want, Beth?"

He knew her instantly. Besides her mother, he was the only one who'd been able to recognize her. Her already pounding heart hammered even harder. She needed to pull herself together. She had little left to lose, but it was important that he understand her deeply personal reasons for the lie. On top of that, Addie had received word that their father would be arriving in Bha'Khar within the week. For Addie's sake it would be best to smooth things over with Malik before then.

"You left this off the palace tour," she said, ignoring the nerves bumping together inside her as she looked around. "Nice office."

It gave her an excuse to sever her gaze from his. Her concentration was scattered, but she had a vague impression of dark wood, bookcases, plush green carpet and a desk littered with papers. This was where he rolled up his sleeves and worked. There was another office where he had photo ops with foreign dignitaries, and held meetings with his ministers.

She couldn't put this off any longer. She wanted to look at him, but she was afraid—because she'd desperately missed him and now she would see only disgust in his expression. When her gaze locked with his, she winced at the hostility smoldering in his dark eyes. Her legs shook, and for the first time she noticed two chairs in front of his desk.

"May I sit?"

He hesitated, clearly conflicted about his answer, but then he finally nodded.

She settled herself and almost regretted the proximity—close enough to smell the familiar spicy fragrance of his aftershave mixed with the wonderful masculine scent of his skin. The combination never failed to stir her senses and now was no exception—however inconvenient it might be to her purpose here.

"I must have a talk with my staff regarding unwanted visitors."

She drew in a sharp breath, but forced herself not to look away. "Don't blame them. I won't make a habit of this."

"Pretending to be someone you are not?" His words were coated with ice.

"Yes." She folded her hands so he wouldn't see them shaking. "It's important that you understand why I did it."

"It will not make a difference to me."

"I've known you to be reasonable and kind. I only ask that you listen to what I have to say."

"Speak quickly."

Beth nodded, wondering how she could sum up so many years of unhappiness and make him understand—quickly.

"Addie and I grew up without our mother, and to all intents and purposes without our father as well. My twin sister is the only person who has ever loved me. Our father is a cold, unfeeling man. He all but ignored me unless he mistook me for Addie and believed I was the twin destined to marry a king."

"Did you deceive him often?"

"I didn't have to." Beth laughed, but there was no humor in the sound. Absently she brushed her fingers over the birthmark on her neck. "He could never tell us apart. When he saw either of us he simply assumed he was looking at Addie. She was the only twin who existed for him."

"Your point?" he asked, leaning back in his leather chair.

Beth saw no change in his cold expression. "Her happiness was not uppermost in his mind."

"Adina told me that she requested you take her place for a short time, and why. But I do not understand *your* motivation for this deception."

"I love her," Beth said simply. "We only ever had each other to count on."

"The fact that you care enough to lie for her has not escaped my notice," he bit out.

"You have no reason to believe this, but I hate lies."

He steepled his fingers together. "You are correct. I do not believe you."

Beth hated that she could understand where he was coming from. He had no reason to think she was any different from the woman who had used him. But he was wrong.

"I told you about the man who lied to me. And before you say anything, it was all true. What I left out, because it was too humiliating, is that a short time after his wedding he called me."

"For what purpose?" The muscle in his jaw jerked.

"He said we shouldn't let a little thing like vows stand in the way of our being together. When I pointed out that it was wrong, he said that his family had political connections and that his own destiny was to take his place in the dynasty. Men like him live by different rules. He asked me to be his mistress, the other woman, part of a lie. It made me sick to my stomach."

Malik's frown deepened. "And yet you eagerly chose to participate in another lie, one that only you could make happen? Only you could have pretended to be my bride."

She looked down at her hands for a moment. "I did it for no other reason than to protect my sister."

"I would not hurt her."

"Not intentionally. I know that now. But I didn't when I agreed to the impersonation. In my experience, powerful men don't care who they hurt to get what they want. How was I to know that you were different? How could I be sure that my sister wouldn't be miserably unhappy and throw her life away? I told the truth about wanting to talk you out of the marriage, because Addie couldn't bear to defy our father and risk rejection from the only parent she had."

"That is no excuse."

She ignored his words. "Now I've come to know that you're an honorable man. And sincere."

And so much more, she thought, memorizing the lean line of his jaw, the dark eyes that could mesmerize her with a single glance, the hands that turned her to a quivering mass of desire with the slightest touch. A part of her regretted the dishonesty. But a deeper part of her would never be sorry that she'd gotten to know him. He had integrity and a keen sense of duty. He was the kind of man she had always longed for.

"Malik, I know you can't understand the deep and abiding bond shared by twins. But you have a brother, and I know you love him. What if Kardahl's happiness was at stake? What if he asked you to do something? To perpetrate a dishonesty that could possibly make the difference between happiness and a lifetime of misery for someone you love?"

"I recall discussing this fundamental principle with you. I said then, and say again now, the wrong thing for the right reason is still wrong."

His eyes didn't soften and his wonderful smile stayed well hidden. Stubborn could be a good quality, but not so much in this case. He hadn't budged; he was unmoved by her words. Honesty and baring her soul had changed nothing. She hadn't let herself consider the possibility that she would fail. The death of hope was a painful pressure in her chest.

Then fear took its place. "What are you going to do?"

"My duty."

"You're going through with the wedding to my sister?" she asked.

"Yes."

She closed her eyes for a moment, drawing air into her lungs. She had to say it. "I know I have no right to ask anything of you, but I'm appealing to the kind and decent man I know you are. Please don't hold this against Addie."

"You are correct. You have no right to ask for anything." He stood, a clear signal that he was finished listening.

Beth reached deep inside herself for the dignity to stand and walk to the door without letting on that she was shaking inside. She put her hand on the knob, then met his gaze.

"You know, Your Highness, it's easy to sit in judgment when you've never had to question your place in the world. It's easy to turn up your nose when you don't have to ask whether anyone loves you or would miss you if you were gone. Taking care of Addie has become a habit for me since our mother disappeared from our lives." She shrugged, and when her hand trembled she gripped the doorknob until her knuckles turned white. "One day she was there, the next day she wasn't. Addie was crying in her bed and I heard her from my room down the hall. I went to her and held her. But Father found me and ordered me out. When I wouldn't leave, he yanked me away from my sister and took me back to my own room. He commanded Addie to stop crying for her mother because she would never see her again." She took a deep, shuddering breath as the memory tightened her chest, then met his gaze. "When my father left to meet whatever woman he was seeing, I sneaked back into my sister's room. I held her and she held me and we cried together."

"I do not see what this has to do with knowingly deceiving me now."

"I'm not going to apologize for protecting my sister. She's all I have. Under the same circumstances I would do it again." Beth lifted her chin a fraction.

"If that makes me a bad person, so be it. And you should count your lucky stars."

"Why is that?"

"If I'd been born two minutes earlier you would be marrying me."

Let him chew on that, she thought, and walked out of his office. The show of guts sustained her until she closed the door. She left the palace in a blur.

He'd known her instantly. Before he could have seen the birthmark.

It's a love thing.

Beth recalled her mother's words. *Love sees beyond superficial features. It has nothing to do with identical features and everything to do with one heart knowing another, knowing the other half of itself.*

The rush of pain was so strong it stole the air from her lungs and made her feelings crystal-clear. She'd found the other half of her heart. But their two hearts would never be one and it was tragically unfair.

She was paying the price for destiny, tradition and her own stupidity. And, as if all that wasn't bad enough, history was repeating itself. This was the second time she'd been devastated by the news that a man was going to marry someone else. But this time it was so much worse. This time she was totally, completely, head-over-heels, he's-the-only-one-for-me in love with a man who would never forgive her.

CHAPTER ELEVEN

"WELCOME home, Mr. Ambassador." The King lifted a glass of champagne, and everyone around the elegantly set circular table in the private palace dining room did the same.

Including Malik.

It was an intimate group—the King and Queen, himself, the ambassador, and his identical twin daughters, one on either side of him. Malik had said nothing of the ruse to his parents. He was certain that the desire to keep her own father from learning of his twins' treachery had prompted Beth's visit to his office.

Malik was not certain what had kept him from revealing the pretense. Part of it was the need to protect his father, who had chosen his bride. The other part was to bear his humiliation in private. Worse than the shame and embarrassment of being duped was the fact that he had not heeded his own warning to stop tender feelings from invading his heart.

He would get over those tender feelings if it took him until his last breath.

Malik refused to look at Beth, and studied her father instead. The older man was dignified, with dark hair graying at the temples. His black eyes were intelligent and shrewd. Of course Malik had met the ambassador on numerous occasions, but knowing him took on more significance since meeting his daughters. The thought sent his gaze to Beth like a magnet to true north.

It had not been his choice to have her at this dinner, and he had attempted to dissuade the Queen. But when she had learned that both of the ambassador's daughters were here there had been no deterring her from this family reunion/welcome home/future in-laws getting acquainted dinner.

Ambassador Rafi Farrah lifted his glass and said, "To my daughter Adina—the future bride of the Crown Prince."

Everyone toasted his wife-to-be. Except Malik. Before learning of the trickery he had pushed to set a wedding date. Fool that he was.

"Malik?"

He met his mother's questioning gaze, then glanced around and noticed everyone but Beth looking at him expectantly.

"To Adina," he said. "May our happiness only be exceeded by our open and honest communication." Malik was looking directly at Beth, and satisfaction shot through him when she winced at his words.

"Worry not, Your Highness," the ambassador said. "She is as obedient as she is beautiful."

The Queen looked at both of them and shook

her head. "Both of your daughters are exceptionally lovely."

"Still, Adina is a jewel among jewels," her father
boasted, then patted Beth's hand.

Malik wondered if the twins had dressed identi-
cally to play games with their father. Or with him.
In his case it was not successful.

"But they look exactly alike," the King said.

Not to me, Malik thought. He had known almost
at once that Adina was not Beth. Kissing her had
been the final proof that she was not the woman he
had come to know and… Love? Self-loathing and re-
crimination consumed him. How could he feel this
intensity of emotion and such profound loss for a
woman who had consciously and deliberately made
a fool of him?

"I agree, Mr. Ambassador," the Queen chimed in.
"How do you tell your daughters apart?"

"It is in the bearing." He looked at Beth and said,
"She will not disappoint, Your Highness. She has
been educated at one of the finest finishing schools
in the world. Her skills in protocol are well polished.
Besides Bha'Kharian and English, she speaks three
other languages fluently. And she can hostess a reception at a moment's notice."

Beth sat up straighter and flashed a look of defiance
at her father. Because Malik had come to know her so
well, he realized that she wanted to say something
sarcastic about her father's arrogant boasting. She
remained silent, however, and he suspected it had more

to do with preserving this moment for her sister than sparing her father's over-inflated ego.

Malik found himself hoping she would lose the battle and say something. He had never realized this flaw of character in the ambassador. Perhaps the man's personality and disposition were beneficial in dealing with other arrogant representatives from countries all over the world, but as a father he was lacking.

Adina put her hand on his arm. "Father, I am grateful for the education you provided. It will be an enormous help in the role I will undertake. And I am looking forward to continuing my education under the guidance of the Queen."

Her Highness smiled. "Another diplomat in the family, Rafi? And what of your other daughter?"

Beth smiled at the King and Queen. "I am a teacher—"

"She is not in the service of Bha'Khar," the ambassador interrupted. "There is nothing of consequence to discuss."

Astonished, Malik watched him brush Beth off as if she were an annoying stain on his shoe, instead of a woman in a noble profession who was worthy of respect. He had listened when she had related the story of her deep, emotional bond with her sister because of her father's abuse of power, but he had not quite believed it until now. He held his tongue out of respect for the King and Queen, but he intended to talk with them privately about this man.

Malik saw something die in Beth's eyes, quickly replaced by resignation, but even that did not completely cover the deep cut of emotional battery. He wanted to shake the stupid, self-important imbecile until he acknowledged that Alina Bethia Farrah was a beautiful, intelligent, spirited woman, and any man would be fortunate to have her in his life.

"But Adina," the ambassador continued, patting her hand now, "can converse with foreign dignitaries from France, Germany and Spain in their own languages."

The lady in question looked most uncomfortable. She glanced at Beth and said, "My sister has a special way of talking to the teenagers she teaches. Some perceive that as a foreign language."

The ambassador shrugged dismissively. "My other daughter would not listen to me. She insisted on a career and refused to wait quietly and patiently for a marriage proposal and the opportunity to make a home for a man. She is not at all like her sister."

"Her gifts are too special to waste," Adina said. "She has the ability to convince her teenage students to embrace and cherish the challenge of learning. It is a revered undertaking."

Beth smiled at her sister, even as a slight shake of her head warned her that pursuing this defense of her character was unwise. Obviously she made a habit of protecting this beloved sister.

Malik found himself in conflict with his feelings. He wanted to stay angry at Beth for what she had done. Yet he found himself admiring her for being a doer in life instead of a spectator.

The ambassador smiled fondly at Adina. "She is the most perfect daughter a man could ask for."

"She is the most perfect sister a sister could ask for," Beth added, standing up for her twin.

Sincerity and love shone in her eyes, in spite of the fact that her selfish, insensitive father had all but ignored her in favor of the twin who would be queen. Leopards did not change their spots, and Malik felt certain it had been that way all her life—as she had told him. The bastard had deprived her of a mother, then pushed her aside as a no one because he aspired to power through the favored daughter betrothed to a future king.

In spite of this Beth had turned out to be a pure-spirited woman who put her sister's welfare above her own. Fears for her sister's happiness had pushed her to pretend, and then to try and convince Malik to be the one to call off the wedding. In that way the father/daughter relationship Adina cherished, for reasons he could not understand, would be preserved. No longer did he consider Beth's actions a flaw in her character, but a courageous quality to be admired.

Malik's gaze was drawn to Beth's face. Was it possible for her to look more miserable? He did not believe so, until she met his gaze and her eyes filled with a soul-deep sorrow. Suddenly his anger evaporated, and when the haze fell away he was left with something bright and beautiful.

He also had a dilemma of national proportions. No Crown Prince in the long and dignified history of Bha'Khar had defied tradition and married a woman of his own choosing simply because he had fallen in love.

* * *

"It's interesting, don't you think, that Mama kept twin beds in her home even though she hasn't seen us since we were little?" Addie rested against several pillows propped against the tufted headboard.

With their switching places discovered, her sister had decided to spend the night on neutral territory.

"It's good to be here with her," Beth agreed, reclining against her identical headboard. A small table with a lamp and a shade trimmed with dangling crystals sat between them.

"I wish I'd known that she was trying to get in touch with us all this time."

Beth smiled. "It's a mom-love thing."

"Speaking of love, could that dinner have been more awkward?"

"It's over," Beth said.

Awkward didn't even begin to describe that dinner from hell, Beth thought. Painful was the first word that came to her mind. Uncomfortable. Unpleasant every time Malik had turned that smoldering gaze in her direction, which had been most of the night. Difficult. Every time she'd looked into his dark eyes, hoping for the familiar friendly gleam, a fresh wave of pain had washed over her when she'd seen that it wasn't there. She would never see it again, nor the spark of desire she'd come to know and look forward to.

"It would have taken a lot to make it more horrible," Beth agreed.

"I'm so sorry I dragged you into this, Bethie."

"That's the last time I want to hear that from you."

She pointed at Addie. "I will support you always. I love you."

"I love you for always being there for me. On the upside, watching Father in action really opened my eyes."

"He was certainly in his element tonight," Beth said bitterly. True to form, he'd all but ignored her except when he'd mixed them up. The rest of the time he'd been a public relations pain in the backside for Addie, the conduit to power. "He was practically rubbing his hands together in glee at the prospect of being related by marriage to the royal family."

"I noticed that, too." Addie's look was solemn. "Do you think the King and Queen know about us switching places?"

Beth thought for a moment, then shook her head. "They were friendly. I've met them a few times since being you, and I would know if anything had changed. For some reason Malik didn't say anything."

Probably because he didn't want them to know he'd been duped again. Beth couldn't blame him. If anyone knew how awful humiliation was, she did.

"Beth, I'm not going to marry Malik."

"What?" Beth slid out of bed and sat on her sister's. "Why, Addie? Is it because you're afraid Malik will be unkind after what we did? He won't. I got to know him pretty well. He'll get over it."

"No, he won't."

He would never treat Addie badly, but Beth knew that because of his past he would never trust her, either.

And a happy marriage needed trust at its foundation. "You're right," she sighed. "He won't get over it."

Addie nodded. "But that's not why I won't marry him."

"You're ready to defy Father?"

"Everything you said came clearly into focus for me tonight. All this time I've been afraid of losing his love. But the way he treated you… Putting you down. Dismissing your accomplishments." Addie frowned. "And making it so clear that he can't wait to be father-in-law to the King of Bha'Khar… Power is what he loves. Not his children." She shook her head. "It made me see that you can't lose what you've never had."

"At least something good came out of this fiasco," Beth said. "Do you want me to go with you to tell Father?"

Addie shook her head. "It's time I grew a spine. I need to fight my own battles and not let you do it for me. In spite of everything, I want him in my life. But if he doesn't understand, then there's nothing I can do about it."

Beth took her sister's hand. "You deserve a chance to find a man who makes you happy. I'm glad you realized before it was too late."

"Me, too." Addie's eyes turned sad. "And what about you?"

"I don't know what you mean."

"Have you found a man who could make you happy?"

Yes. But she'd burned that bridge.

Instead of answering, she said, "Don't you worry about me, Addie."

"Oh, please. Like that would work if I said it to you. Of *course* I worry about you. It's part of the reason I'm willing to take on Father."

"What are you talking about?"

"I can't marry the man you're in love with."

Beth shook her head. "You're wrong—"

"Don't go there, sis. I know you better than anyone. I saw the way you looked at Malik. You are *so* gone over him."

"Even if you're right—which I'm not saying you are—your whole life has been spent in training to become the Queen of Bha'Khar. You've planned and studied. You're demure and docile. I'm straightforward and sarcastic. Besides the fact that there's not a snowball's chance in hell that Malik can get over what I've done to him, I couldn't be more wrong to be the King's wife."

"You can learn."

"I could. But why? He hates me."

"That's not what I saw," Addie said, crossing her arms over her chest as she leaned back against her headboard. "He couldn't keep his eyes off you tonight."

"Probably picturing three hundred ways to kill me with his bare hands," she mumbled.

Addie laughed. "Don't be dramatic."

"I'm not."

"The thing is, Bethie, I'm not doing it just for you. I couldn't marry a man who's in love with another woman."

"Of course not. That would be asking for trouble. But Malik is—"

"He's in love with you."

Beth met her gaze and knew there was something worse than the heartrending pain of loss. It was hope. It was lying to herself with the possibility that she had a chance with Malik when deep inside she knew that could never be. Her sin was too big.

"No."

Addie took her hand. "He knew practically right away that I wasn't you."

"So he can tell us apart? He's a highly intelligent man."

"So is Father, and he never gets it right."

Beth shrugged. "He might have had a soft spot for me for a little while, but it's too late now. There's no way Malik will ever trust me."

"They say love conquers all," Addie pointed out.

"I've been foolish in the past, and it shames me," Beth said, looking down at her hands. "I won't be foolish enough to believe that."

She'd found out the hard way that honesty was the best policy. As badly as she wanted to believe that Malik could love her as much as she loved him, she knew it was impossible. He would never understand why she'd lied. Without that, there was no way to atone for what she'd done to him. She had to be honest with herself and face the truth.

There would be no happy ending for her.

CHAPTER TWELVE

AFTER a sleepless night that even the finest brandy in the world had not prevented, Malik decided he must speak to his father. He had made up his mind, and it was best not to put off what would be a difficult conversation. Malik barged into the King's office, disregarding his secretary and all attempts to bar the way.

"Father, I must speak with you. The matter is of urgent importance."

The young man who had insinuated himself between father and son in the pursuit of his duty looked distressed. "Your Highness, I tried to stop him, but—"

Reading glasses sitting on the end of his nose, the King looked up. "This cannot wait, Malik?"

"No, Father."

He set the glasses on his desk and smiled at his secretary. "It is all right, Sharif. Leave us."

"Very well, Your Highness."

When they were alone Malik looked around the office. It was much like his own, but larger. Dark furniture, plush carpet, priceless paintings adorning the walls, and an ornate curio cabinet with an exquisite display of the finest glass artwork.

"Are you trying to decide where to put your desk when you take over this office upon my retirement?"

Malik met his father's amused gaze. "That is part of what I have come to speak with you about."

"Do sit down, then, my boy. Hastening the transfer of power is quite an urgent matter."

"I am in no hurry to accelerate your departure from your duties," Malik amended. "But I have come to seek your counsel regarding a related issue."

The King leaned forward and rested his arms on his desk. The sleeves of his white dress shirt were rolled up and his tie loosened, though it was only mid-morning. Malik had always admired his father's work ethic and tried to emulate him. He was an exceptional ruler and his shoes would not be easy to fill. Malik had sought to prove that when he took over the throne the people of Bha'Khar would be in good hands. He wanted to make his father proud. He had only stumbled a few times, but what he had to say now would no doubt make previous missteps pale in comparison.

"What is it, my son? And, before you begin, may I say that you look dreadful?"

"I do not doubt it. Sleep has been elusive since my *betrothed* arrived."

"She is a lovely young woman. The Queen and I have discussed the situation, and she is convinced that there is a romantic spark between you."

The Queen was, of course, referring to Beth, and

"spark" did not begin to describe how he felt. Inferno was more to the point. Feelings for her burned through him with an intensity he had never before experienced.

"There is a spark," Malik admitted.

His father's smile was pleased. "Excellent."

"Not so much."

"Why do you say that?"

"She is not my betrothed."

"I do not understand. Of course she is."

Malik shook his head. "You yourself said that she and her twin look exactly alike and you could not tell them apart."

"Their likeness to each other is quite amazing. But that does not explain why your attraction is not an excellent thing."

"The woman I have come to know—the woman I believed all this time to be named in the marriage contract, the woman who generates romantic sparks—is not the woman I am supposed to marry. The twins switched places."

It was fascinating to watch the King process the words. Shocked realization was reflected on his face. "Beth is not your betrothed?"

"No. She assumed the role because her sister asked her to do so." After looking at the ambassador through Beth's eyes, Malik admitted that in her place he would have had reservations, too. "It was the wrong thing for the right reason."

The King frowned. "I disagree."

Malik recalled feeling the same, and chiding her

about that very thing. In his own arrogance he had stated with utter conviction that there was never a good enough reason to do the wrong thing. He regretted those words and wished he could take them back.

"I have come to know her heart. I do not believe she is in the habit of deception."

"And yet the pretense was seamless? She passed herself off as the woman you are to marry? How are we to believe she is not a skilled manipulator?"

"Father, I am aware that the ambassador is one of your oldest friends. But last night I looked at him through eyes opened by his daughter."

"How so?"

"Her father is using his firstborn daughter to solidify his influence with you. Beth was concerned that the sister she loves was being used to further her father's selfish motives. She did what she thought was right."

"She did not tell the truth. How can that be right?"

"I know without any doubt that she is not in the habit of being deceitful." He stood and looked down at his father. "I cannot explain to you how I have come to believe in her, but there is no doubt in my mind that her intentions were pure. I do not condone her actions, but I cannot fault her for them, either."

"How can you say this?"

He set his hands on the desk and met his father's gaze. "Your Highness, I have great respect for your wisdom. I have learned from the best. But hear me well. I will not listen to criticism of Beth. You must trust my judgment."

"You are in love with her." It was not a question.

"Yes." Malik straightened and ran a hand through his hair. "Once I believed that I could not fulfill my responsibilities as a ruler if love distracted me."

"And now?" The King's eyes narrowed.

"Now I believe just the opposite is true. From the time I was a mere boy you have counseled that the King cannot tolerate distractions. I have tried to heed your words. But without Beth by my side, for support, counsel, humor and love, I do not believe that I can be a wise and effective ruler. I do not have faith that I can follow you and lead Bha'Khar into a position of strength and significance in the global community. I cannot be the kind of King my people expect and deserve."

His father considered Malik's words for many moments without any indication of his feelings. Finally he said, "Love is never a distraction, but a gift. If I have somehow misled you to believe that leadership and love are mutually exclusive, I must beg your forgiveness."

"You are not to blame. My own foolish actions are responsible."

"You are referring to the duplicitous journalist?" The King sighed. "One cannot go through life mistrusting everyone, my son. Your judgment is sound. Trust yourself, as I have learned to trust in you. You must make decisions based on what your heart tells you to do."

"That is why I have come," Malik said. "I cannot marry the woman you have chosen for me."

"I see." The King rested his elbows on the arms of his chair and steepled his fingers. "And?"

"Kardahl followed tradition and was fortunate enough to find love with his betrothed. It is only fitting that I step aside and allow my brother to assume the leadership of Bha'Khar in my stead."

"You would give up the throne for Beth? She means that much to you?" his father asked.

"She means everything to me," he said simply.

Malik had not allowed himself to articulate his feelings in those terms until that moment. But the words were true, and he meant them to his soul. The why of it wasn't important. How he had come to this place did not matter. It was a fact he embraced with every part of his being. He would give up all that he had to have Beth in his life.

"I see."

"I apologize for disappointing you, Father. There are no excuses, and I would not speak about them regardless. You have every right to be angry."

"Is Beth in love with you?"

"I do not know."

It was better than admitting the truth. He had refused to listen. If she had loved him, it was over now. His chest tightened. He did not like the sensation, but there seemed to be little choice except learning to live with it.

"And yet you would give up your right to be King for this woman?"

"Not for her. I would step aside because I would

rather be alone than wed another simply for the sake of tradition."

"As your King, I would say that tradition should not be ignored. But the father in me only wishes your happiness."

"The two are in conflict," Malik pointed out. "The only resolution is for me to step aside."

"Do not be so hasty, my son. There may be another solution."

Fighting tears, Beth checked the chest of drawers one last time for anything she might have missed, before zipping her suitcase closed and setting it on the floor. It seemed wrong that she was going home tomorrow with the same amount of luggage she'd brought to Bha'Khar, since she was returning to the States with far more baggage. Emotional baggage. And she couldn't shake the feeling that she was forgetting something.

Oh, yes. She was leaving her heart behind.

The irony didn't escape her. She'd perpetuated this pretense to protect her sister's tender heart from the Crown Prince and had fallen for him herself. Stupid. Stupid. *Stupid.* She couldn't even say she'd lost him, because there had never been a chance of having him.

There was a soft knock on the door just before Sameera opened it. She sighed when she saw the suitcases lined up. "Beth?"

"Hi, Mom." Her own sadness was compounded when she saw the same emotion in her mother's eyes.

"I wish you would reconsider your decision to leave. Bha'Khar could use your teaching skills. I could use your—" Her voice caught. "I just do not want you to go. It pains me that you will be halfway around the world again."

Beth hugged her. "Me, too. But look on the bright side. We found each other, and now we can keep in touch. E-mail. And when I need to hear your voice I can pick up the phone."

Sameera touched her cheek tenderly, and a pleading expression darkened her black eyes. "And you will visit?"

That was a hard one to answer. Bha'Khar held mostly bad memories. Malik believed Beth to be a liar, but in truth she was exceptionally unskilled at hiding the truth.

"You can visit me in the States," Beth suggested.

"Yes, I can do that." Her look was fierce and determined. "No one will keep me from my children ever again."

"And no one can keep me from my mother," Beth vowed, pressing her hand over the one Sameera held to her cheek. When she'd succeeded in surrounding her tender heart with calluses, she would visit Bha'Khar again.

"Good. Now, let us not spend your last night here being melancholy. I have prepared a nice dinner. It will be ready in about an hour. And I have a nice bottle of wine."

"I'd like that."

"Your sister will be here in a little while. To share your last night before you go away."

"I'm curious to know what Malik said when she told him the wedding was off."

Sameera frowned. "We will not have to wait long."

Her mother refused help as she put the finishing touches on the meal, and Beth was shooed out of the kitchen with a glass of white wine in her hand. The doorbell rang and she opened it to her sister.

"Hi."

Addie hugged her, then pointed to the glass in her hand. "Is there more of that?"

Beth heard an odd tone in her voice and noticed her sister looked nervous. "Are you all right?"

"Fine."

"What happened with Malik?"

"It was all good." Addie's gaze shifted away.

"Then why are you acting weird? What's wrong?"

"Nothing. I'd just like a glass of wine." She started toward the kitchen. "You need to turn on the news."

Puzzled, Beth did as she'd asked. "I live to serve…."

She sat in the tiny room off the kitchen that was used for the television and picked up the remote. A newscast was just starting, and there was a flash on the screen about a breaking story. Addie and Sameera joined her a few minutes later and sat on the sofa, one on each side of her.

The beautiful dark-haired, exotic-eyed news anchor announced that the studio had just received videotape from the palace. Seconds later Malik's face appeared on the screen. Beth's heart caught and a fist squeezed inside her. For long moments she could forget, then one glance at the love she'd lost brought all the pain roaring back.

"I'll go check dinner," she said, starting to rise.

Addie grabbed her arm. "Stay. Watch."

Malik was reading from a prepared statement. "It will be my humble honor to serve the people of Bha'Khar when my father retires. Part of my duty is to marry the woman chosen by the King. This tradition has been successful for a very long time, but selecting a bride is not like picking out a piece of fruit. The King shares my opinion that the time has come to change tradition and allow the Crown Prince to choose a bride who suits him in every way."

The doorbell rang again, and they all started. Her mother said, "I am not expecting anyone else. Who could that be?"

Beth watched her sister take a large swallow of wine. "Addie?"

"Do I look psychic?" she asked.

"You still look like something's wrong."

The doorbell rang more insistently, and Sameera stood. "Someone has picked a very bad time to visit."

"Addie, what's going on?" she asked when they were alone.

"You heard Malik. He's going to do away with the royal tradition of betrothal."

"Was he furious about you calling it off?" She looked at her sister. "Are you okay?"

Addie smiled with genuine pleasure. "I'm fine.

Better than fine. It's like a weight has been lifted from my shoulders. And Malik was gracious and understanding."

"Did you know about this?" Beth asked.

Addie shook her head. "I knew something was up, because of the media at the palace, but not the details of the announcement."

Shock didn't begin to describe her feelings. Beth stared at her sister.

"Beth?" The familiar deep voice drew her gaze to the doorway, where Malik stood. He walked over and sat beside her.

How did he do that? she wondered. How did he know her from her identical twin? She looked around and realized that her mother and sister had left them alone.

He looked at the TV screen, then picked up the remote and shut it off. "There is something I wish to discuss with you."

"I saw what you did."

"Yes. And?" He was looking at her expectantly.

"And—what the heck are you thinking?"

"I am thinking that I wish to choose for myself the woman I will spend the rest of my life with."

"Was the King very angry?" she asked, afraid for him. Afraid to really look at the ramifications of his actions.

"Changing tradition was his idea."

"But why?"

"Because he knew that I would not be happy with his choice."

She pressed a hand to his forehead. "No fever."

"Perhaps not, but I burn for you."

She wanted to believe. But what if he wasn't saying what she thought he was saying? What if he was just telling her that pretending to be his bride had annihilated hundreds of years of tradition and her name would go down in the history of Bha'Khar as the woman who had single-handedly dealt tradition the death blow? It was easier to believe the bad stuff than hope for her heart's desire, only to have it snatched away.

"How can you feel that way when you know I'm a liar?"

"There were extenuating circumstances."

"I'm not a docile woman."

"I am aware of that. I do not want a docile woman. I want you."

"Why?" she couldn't help asking.

"You taught me the meaning of love." He took her cold hands in his warm ones. "It is clear to me that deceit is not natural to you, and you despise dishonesty as much as I. Love was the reason for your actions." He shrugged, as if that explained everything. "Challenge does not only build character, it reveals it. I have learned your character. When someone you love is facing a crisis, you will do whatever is necessary—including going against your core belief to protect a loved one. I hope that I fall into that esteemed group."

"Fall into it? You're the leader."

Intensity darkened his eyes and his hands gripped hers more firmly. "Does that mean you love me?"

"With all my heart, I'm afraid," she answered, before her throat grew tight and tears burned her eyes.

He was right. She couldn't lie, even though telling him the truth had just laid bare her most tender secret.

He touched a finger to her chin, nudging it up so she met his gaze. "Do not be afraid, my sweet. You are the woman who does not fear doing the wrong thing for the right reason. You are the one I want at my side for the rest of my life."

"You changed tradition for *me*?" The magnitude of his gesture overwhelmed her. She'd shunned powerful men, but power was as power did. He'd used his for good. Actions spoke louder than words, and his showed what was in his heart.

"My motives are selfish, but my reasoning is sound. The pressures of a leader are great."

"Speaking of leaders," she said, tilting her head as she looked up at him. "It occurs to me that my father is not going to be happy about this."

A muscle in Malik's jaw went tight. "He will accept my choice with grace and he will treat you with respect. If he does not, his appointment as ambassador can easily be revoked."

"Or he could be transferred to Antarctica. Does Bha'Khar conduct diplomatic relations there?"

He grinned. "I like the way you think. Which is why I have no doubt you are the right one, and why I need you so. It takes someone special to help bear the royal burden. And you are the most special woman I have ever met."

"I have no training to be Queen. I can't promise perfection."

"Anyone can learn royal duties. But you are the only perfect wife for me. I will assume the throne of Bha'Khar soon, and I wish to do that with you as my queen. For you are already the ruler of my heart."

She pressed her fingers to her lips as happiness gathered inside her. "Oh, Malik— I don't know what to say."

He went down on one knee and pulled a ring from the pocket of his pants. "Say that you will marry me."

"I will."

"This was my great-grandmother's." He slid onto her finger an emerald and diamond ring, the most beautiful thing she had ever seen. After pulling her to her feet, and into his arms, he kissed her until her toes curled. When he lifted his head she met his gaze, amazed that she could be so happy when she had believed she would never be happy again.

"Your Highness…"

"I do love it when you call me that."

She smiled. "Honesty compels me to tell you that being Queen doesn't thrill me. However, I love you very, very much, and since you're going to be King it kind of goes with the territory. All I really want is to be your wife. And a royal baby would be the icing on the royal cake."

"A child with his mother's spirit and integrity?" He thought for a moment. "Actually, I wish to have twins. After dealing me double the trouble, the least destiny can do is multiply the joy."

"I couldn't agree more."

He kissed her again, a joining of lips that sealed their promises and left no room for anything but the truth. Beth knew Malik loved her fully and completely, and being his wife was all she wanted. This agreement was more binding than any flimsy piece of paper. It was between her sheikh and his bride— a contract of two hearts that through a quirk of fate had become one.

* * * * *

THE ROYAL HOUSE OF NIROLI
Always passionate, always proud

The richest royal family in the world—united by
blood and passion,
torn apart by deceit and desire

Nestled in the azure blue of the Mediterranean Sea, the
majestic island of Niroli has prospered for centuries.
The Fierezza men have worn the crown with passion
and pride since ancient times. But now, as the king's
health declines, and his two sons have been tragically
killed, the crown is in jeopardy.

The clock is ticking—a new heir must be found
before the king is forced to abdicate. By royal decree
the internationally scattered members of the Fierezza
family are summoned to claim their destiny. But any
person who takes the throne must do so according to
The Rules of the Royal House of Niroli. Soon secrets
and rivalries emerge as the descendents of this ancient
royal line vie for position and power. Only a true
Fierezza can become ruler—a person dedicated to their
country, their people…and their eternal love!

*Each month starting in July 2007,
Harlequin Presents is delighted to bring you
an exciting installment from*
THE ROYAL HOUSE OF NIROLI,
*in which you can follow the epic search
for the true Nirolian king.
Eight heirs, eight romances, eight fantastic stories!*

Here's your chance to enjoy a sneak preview of the
first book delivered to you by royal decree…

FIVE minutes later she was standing immobile in front of the study's window, her original purpose of coming in forgotten, as she stared in shocked horror at the envelope she was holding. Waves of heat followed by icy chill surged through her body. She could hardly see the address now through her blurred vision, but the crest on its left-hand front corner stood out, its *royal* crest, followed by the address: *HRH Prince Marco of Niroli...*

She didn't hear Marco's key in the apartment door, she didn't even hear him calling out her name. Her shock was so great that nothing could penetrate it. It encased her in a kind of bubble, which only concentrated the torment of what she was suffering and branded it on her brain so that it could never be forgotten. It was only finally pierced by the sudden opening of the study door as Marco walked in.

"Welcome home, *Your Highness*. I suppose I ought to curtsy." She waited, praying that he would laugh and tell her that she had got it all wrong, that the envelope she was holding, addressing him as Prince Marco of Niroli, was some silly mistake. But like a tiny candle flame shivering vulnerably in the dark, her hope trembled fearfully. And then the look in Marco's eyes extinguished it as cruelly as a hand placed callously over a dying person's face to stem their last breath.

"Give that to me," he demanded, taking the envelope from her.

"It's too late, Marco," Emily told him brokenly. "I know the truth now…." She dug her teeth in her lower lip to try to force back her own pain.

"You had no right to go through my desk," Marco shot back at her furiously, full of loathing at being caught off-guard and forced into a position in which he was in the wrong, making him determined to find something he could accuse Emily of. "I trusted you…."

Emily could hardly believe what she was hearing. "No, you didn't trust me, Marco, and you didn't trust me because you knew that I couldn't trust you. And you knew that because you're a liar, and liars don't trust people because they know that they themselves cannot be trusted." She not only felt sick, she also felt as though she could hardly breathe. "You are Prince Marco of Niroli…. How could you not tell me who you are and still live with me as intimately as we have lived together?" she demanded brokenly.

"Stop being so ridiculously dramatic," Marco demanded fiercely. "You are making too much of the situation."

"*Too much?*" Emily almost screamed the words at him. "When were you going to tell me, Marco? Perhaps you just planned to walk away without telling me anything? After all, what do my feelings matter to you?"

"Of course they matter." Marco stopped her sharply. "And it was in part to protect them, and you, that I decided not to inform you when my grandfather first announced that he intended to step down from the throne and hand it on to me."

"To protect me?" Emily nearly choked on her fury. "Hand on the throne? No wonder you told me when you first took me to bed that all you wanted was sex. You *knew* that was the only kind of relationship there could ever be between us! You *knew* that one day you would be Niroli's king. No doubt you are expected to marry a princess. Is she picked out for you already, your *royal* bride?"

* * * * *

Look for
THE FUTURE KING'S PREGNANT MISTRESS
by Penny Jordan in July 2007,
from Harlequin Presents,
available wherever books are sold.

HARLEQUIN®

Mediterranean NIGHTS™

Experience the glamour and elegance of cruising the high seas with a new 12-book series....

MEDITERRANEAN NIGHTS

Coming in July 2007...

SCENT OF A WOMAN

by

Joanne Rock

When Danielle Chevalier is invited to an exclusive conference aboard *Alexandra's Dream,* she knows it will mean good things for her struggling fragrance company. But her dreams get a setback when she meets Adam Burns, a representative from a large American conglomerate.

Danielle is charmed by the brusque American— until she finds out he means to compete with her bid for the opportunity that will save her family business!

HM38961

THE GARRISONS

A brand-new family saga begins with

THE CEO'S SCANDALOUS AFFAIR

BY ROXANNE ST. CLAIRE

Eldest son Parker Garrison is preoccupied running his Miami hotel empire and dealing with his recently deceased father's secret second family. Since he has little time to date, taking his superefficient assistant to a charity event should have been a simple plan. Until passion takes them beyond business.

Don't miss any of the six exciting titles in **THE GARRISONS** continuity, beginning in July. Only from Silhouette Desire.

THE CEO'S SCANDALOUS AFFAIR

#1807

Available July 2007.

HARLEQUIN *Presents*

THE ROYAL HOUSE OF NIROLI

Always passionate, always proud.

**The richest royal family in the world—
a family united by blood and passion,
torn apart by deceit and desire.**

Step into the glamorous, enticing world of the
Nirolian Royal Family. As the king ails he must find an
heir…each month an exciting new installment follows
the epic search for the true Nirolian king. Eight heirs,
eight romances, eight fantastic stories!

It's time for playboy prince Marco Fierezza to
claim his rightful place…on the throne of Niroli!
Emily loves Marco, but she has no idea he's a royal
prince! What will this king-in-waiting do when he
discovers his mistress is pregnant?

THE FUTURE KING'S PREGNANT MISTRESS

by Penny Jordan

(#2643)

On sale July 2007.

REQUEST YOUR FREE BOOKS!
2 FREE NOVELS PLUS 2
FREE GIFTS!

HARLEQUIN ROMANCE

From the Heart, For the Heart

YES! Please send me 2 FREE Harlequin Romance® novels and my 2 FREE gifts. After receiving them, if I don't wish to receive any more books, I can return the shipping statement marked "cancel." If I don't cancel, I will receive 4 brand-new novels every month and be billed just $3.57 per book in the U.S., or $4.05 per book in Canada, plus 25¢ shipping and handling per book and applicable taxes, if any*. That's a savings of over 15% off the cover price! I understand that accepting the 2 free books and gifts places me under no obligation to buy anything. I can always return a shipment and cancel at any time. Even if I never buy another book from Harlequin, the two free books and gifts are mine to keep forever.

114 HDN EEV7 314 HDN EEWK

Name _____ (PLEASE PRINT)

Address _____ Apt. _____

City _____ State/Prov. _____ Zip/Postal Code _____

Signature (if under 18, a parent or guardian must sign)

Mail to the **Harlequin Reader Service®**:
IN U.S.A.: P.O. Box 1867, Buffalo, NY 14240-1867
IN CANADA: P.O. Box 609, Fort Erie, Ontario L2A 5X3

Not valid to current Harlequin Romance subscribers.

Want to try two free books from another line?
Call 1-800-873-8635 or visit www.morefreebooks.com.

* Terms and prices subject to change without notice. NY residents add applicable sales tax. Canadian residents will be charged applicable provincial taxes and GST. This offer is limited to one order per household. All orders subject to approval. Credit or debit balances in a customer's account(s) may be offset by any other outstanding balance owed by or to the customer. Please allow 4 to 6 weeks for delivery.

Your Privacy: Harlequin is committed to protecting your privacy. Our Privacy Policy is available online at www.eHarlequin.com or upon request from the Reader Service. From time to time we make our lists of customers available to reputable firms who may have a product or service of interest to you. If you would prefer we not share your name and address, please check here. ☐

HR07